Part Two

The Obsession Series

BROOKE PAGE

Part Two
The Obsession Series

Copyright 2015 by Brooke Page

WARNING

The following story contains mature themes and sexual situations. It is intended for adult readers.

Edited By: Jennifer Hall
Cover Design By: Designs By Dana

TABLE OF CONTENTS

CHAPTER ONE

"Hey," Nathan's voice startled me as I finally breathed when I laid eyes on him. His brows furrowed with worry. "You okay?"

He entered the elevator, and once the doors closed, I reached for him, squeezing him with all that I had while silent tears fell. "It's okay," he said soothingly, rubbing his hands on my bare back. I must have looked horrible, but I was so thankful that my other best friend was here. I might not be able to see him again if I needed to run from Rod.

"Can I take you somewhere?" he asked gently, his hand running through my hair. He pulled a pin from it, one Mitch must have missed last night. "Jesus, Jay. What's going on?" he asked, flicking the pin to the ground. "I've never seen you like this."

I laughed. *If only he knew how fucked up I really was.* "Can you take me home, please?"

He nodded, keeping an arm firmly around my waist as we walked out of the elevator. My eyes grazed the crowds of finely dressed people in this fancy hotel. I was thankful Nathan looked put together in his chino's and polo shirt. Maybe everyone would stare at him instead of the train wreck look I was sporting.

"I'll drop you, then come back here to get my things. Then we can head to the airport and catch a flight on standby if you'd like?" he questioned, tipping the valet.

I nodded, grateful for his friendship. "Don't leave, your family's here. Be with them. I need to see my family." If Rod were here, seeing my family would be safe for once. They always offered me some type of solace when I was feeling lost and out of ideas. Besides, the twin's birthday party was supposed to be tomorrow. It'd make my mother's month if I'd show up for the event.

"Everything okay with them?" he asked as we pulled out of the hotel.

I blinked for a moment, forgetting what I'd just told him. "Yes, well, my father isn't feeling well." I lied, not wanting to share my troubles with Nathan.

"Call me if you need anything, Jay. Kobiashi can pull strings at any hospital in that state."

I nodded, guilt filling me for lying to him. "I'll drive myself to the airport. I've got my Jeep here still, don't worry about it."

He studied me, then nodded back. "Text me when you get there."

CHAPTER TWO

Jamie, Age 17.

"Here." Landon handed me a glass of sprite. I'd barely left my room, saying I had the stomach flu. My mother was worried, and threatening to take me to the hospital if I couldn't get up and move by tomorrow morning.

"Thanks," I whispered, taking a sip. The fizz burned my throat, and reminding me of Rod's hands as he tried to strangle the life from me. A tear rolled down my cheek and didn't go unnoticed by Landon.

"Please, let me talk to Dad," he begged. He'd hovered around me as much as he could without my parents noticing. "You don't have to be afraid anymore."

"Until I find out I'm carrying his monster," I choked, rolling over and burrowing my head under the covers.

Landon's hand found my hip. "We'll get rid of it, Jay. He'll never know."

For some reason, I had a feeling Rod already knew, and the sick, twisted bastard probably did it on purpose. I always had to be the one to remember the condom, and he rarely put them on unless I demanded it.

"You're going to have to go back to school soon. Especially when mom takes you to the doctor and they find nothing is wrong, or they figure out you're pregnant."

"We don't know if I'm pregnant," I snapped, uncovering my head from the blankets. "I'll go tomorrow." I gulped, realizing where else I had to go. "I have to work too."

Landon stood up and muttered, "Jamie, you can't work with him!"

"I can't avoid him, either!" I needed to somehow make him understand we weren't going to be together, and threaten that I'd tell my Dad, without actually telling my Dad I sighed to myself. Rod knew me too well. He knew I'd never be able to disappoint him.

"I'm sitting in the parking lot the whole time, and I swear to God if he makes one wrong move—"

"Fine," I conceded. "It'll be fine." I wasn't sure if I were trying to convince Landon or myself. "I need to shower and get ready for dinner now."

Landon watched me stand, our similar brown eyes stormy, yet scared of the unknown.

***

"You sure about this?" Landon asked as we pulled into the station.

I nodded. I was dressed to impress, ready to take on this asshole by playing mind games with him. I was done being his puppet, and he needed to know I wasn't going to put up with his shit anymore. Landon wasn't as tense either, and I believe it was my confidence. He knew I'd get him if I couldn't handle it.

Wrapping the fashionable scarf tightly around my collar that Landon bought to cover the bruises on my neck, I stepped out of the car, ready to bring the wrath to Rod. That wrath included pepper spray if he got handsy. Landon pulled into a parking spot, taking out his Air Force notes. His test was coming up, and this extra bit of time to study was a blessing in disguise.

But before I entered the station, my father came rushing out. His large frame was the size of the door threshold, and I stopped in my tracks when I saw the murderous look in his eyes. Once he saw me, his head dipped low as he bit the sides of his cheeks.

At that moment, I knew he knew, and the shame and guilt over-powered me.

"Let's go," he said in a low tone as he passed me. I couldn't move as my lip quivered, realizing I was in a whole heap of trouble.

Landon's car door opened and closed. "Dad? What happened?"

"Take your sister home and stay there. Tell your mother I'll be late and not to worry about me for dinner."

"Is everything okay?"

"Do as I say!" my father shouted at Landon, making both of us wince. He wasn't a man to mess with. Criminals cowered whenever they saw him at the station.

I still hadn't moved, then noticed Rod standing in the door frame, smug look on his face with his arms crossed as he watched me. He wasn't supposed to see my tears, but they danced on my eyelashes.

"Get in the car with Landon, Jamie," my father commanded, but I still couldn't move. I heard a heavy sigh as I stared down at my feet. Crinkling of gravel got closer, then my father was standing in front of me, blocking Rod from my sight. "This is my fault, sweetheart. Go home with Landon. I'm making it go away."

I closed my eyes, covering them with my hands as I silently sobbed. He wrapped his arms around me, cradling me as he walked me to the car. "It'll be our secret," he said quietly before we reached Landon. I nodded, figuring he thought Landon didn't know. Guilt still filled me, knowing I'd be making my father keep things from my mother, something no marriage should have.

CHAPTER THREE

"Hey, it's Jamie!" my mother shrieked as I walked through the front door of their house. It was smaller than the house I'd grown up in. We moved my senior year, but my family had made it a home, and I always had a couch to sleep on if I needed it. But I wouldn't stay long, not with Rod on a wild goose chase coming after me.

I'd ignored my phone, knowing Mitch would be calling and texting me constantly. I'd left him naked and wanting me, something I felt awful for doing, but I knew it was in his best interest.

My arms wrapped around my mother as she greeted me on two bouncy feet. "I'm so glad you could make it home for the twins!" She held me close, and I felt her love surround me. "Come on, all the family is in the back!"

I grinned as I followed her through the house. I stopped at Landon's picture on the wall. He looked so proud after receiving his Air Force recognition and uniform for the first time. My mother noticed, wrapping her arm around me.

"I wish he could be here today too," she said with a smile, kissing me on the cheek. I nodded, then moved to the kitchen, hugging Riley the second I saw her. She was helping my mother prep food, and I was happy to see her being useful.

"Jamie!" Riley squealed, jumping up and down before she hugged me.

I laughed at her greeting but held her close.

Trevor walked over, he was almost thirteen, and I knew hugging wasn't cool anymore, so I tapped his hat in greeting. He gave me a mischievous smile, and it pulled at my heart. He looked so much like Landon, and that smile reminded me of Mitch now as well, making my heart crush even more.

"There's my shining star!" my father greeted me as he walked through the sliding door. He was wearing his 'Kiss the Cook' apron while holding a tray full of hot dogs and hamburgers.

"Hi, Dad." I smiled, kissing his cheek so he wouldn't try to hug me while holding the plate of food. "How can I help?" I asked, easily sliding into the normal routine of my crazy family.

***

"A remote helicopter!" Collin yelled as he tore open his gift. Jacob was doing the same, jumping up and down when he realized he got one too.

"Thanks, Jamie!" they both exclaimed simultaneously. Collin lunged at me for a hug, then Jacob followed.

"Why'd you make us wait?" Collin asked as he ran back to the box, trying to rip it open with his nail.

"I wanted to surprise you. Besides, this is from all of your siblings, not just me." I winked at my mother, who gave me a thankful smile. She didn't like it when I'd spend a lot of money on them, but at the same time she knew I wanted to.

"Well, it's so cool. Almost as cool as the Xbox from Mom and Dad!" I grinned, but inside I felt terrible. I knew those were expensive, and my Dad probably worked overtime to get it for them.

"And that was a gift for Trevor, too," my Dad added, slapping Trevor on the back while they sat next to each other on the couch. Trevor gave him a grateful smile, eagerness in his eyes. I'm sure he was chomping at the bit to be done with family time and go play on the game system with his little brothers.

"Does that mean for my birthday I'll get to go to cheer camp?" Riley asked with skepticism. My father's face fell. I knew they wanted to buy us everything, but some things were just too expensive.

"We'll see, sweetie," my mother said nonchalantly, running her hand through Riley's hair. Her face fell, but she still held a smile. She understood my parents' financial situation. Thankfully, she didn't know I was the one who had caused it.

A knock came on the door. "That must be Sharon. She's picking up an order." My mother jumped from her seat on the floor heading for the door. I was happy her jewelry sales business was doing decent. It made her feel good that she could contribute.

"What games do you want for the Xbox?" I asked Trevor as the twins brought their helicopters to Dad to help open.

"Jamie, there's someone at the door for you," my mother said, coming back into the room. I stood, not sure who would be here to see me. I didn't have any friends back home. "Not to mention a very attractive someone," my mother whispered as I walked by. My eyes widened, and so did Riley's.

She turned on the couch, looking through the blinds. "Oh my God! Who is that?" Riley nearly panted. My brows crinkled as I stepped closer to the door, my body wanting to curl into the fetal position when I saw Mitch through the screen door.

He looked beat up and miserable, but his eyes held relief when they saw me. Guilt overwhelmed me, knowing I'd caused him to worry. "What are you doing here?" I said in a harsh whisper while closing both the screen and front door. "How did you find me?"

"Your parents' address is on your emergency contact list. Nathan told me you were coming here." His eyes became darker. "You left me without saying goodbye. One minute we were kissing naked in bed, then the next you booked it while I was in the shower. What the hell, Jamie?"

I owed him an explanation, but I didn't know what to say. "You look terrible."

"That's because my stomach's been in knots wondering what happened to you. Why the hell didn't you just tell me your dad was sick and you needed to come home?"

"I didn't think it'd be a big deal." I fidgeted, moving my hair behind my ears trying to buy time. I noticed Riley watching us with curious eyes. I rolled mine, then grabbed Mitch's hand, leading him in front of the garage where she couldn't see us.

"Jamie, what's going on?" he asked.

"At first I thought my dad was sick, but my mother made it sound worse than what it was," I lied, pissed at myself for telling Nathan that stupid lie.

Mitch ran his hands over his short sandy hair in frustration. "You ran from me."

"No," I scoffed, shifting my weight from leg to leg.

He scowled at me, obviously frustrated with my reply. "You going to invite me in?"

"What?"I was baffled by his question. "Why?"

"It's a party, I'd think your family might want to know who's interrupting it."

"The party's actually over."

Mitch's green eyes widened in frustration.

"Jamie, why don't you invite your friend inside? We've got plenty of leftovers!" my mother said, coming around the corner.

"Hi, I'm Mitch." My mother took Mitch's hand. If I didn't know any better, I'd say she was swooning over him. "I'd love something to eat. I've been traveling all day."

"Jamie, don't be rude. Invite him inside," my mother chastised.

I tried to contain my eye roll, knowing my mother would scold me the second she saw me doing it. "Mitch, would you like to come inside?" I grumbled.

"As a matter of fact, I'd love that." His teeth shown through in his smile, and I wanted to deck him. My mother urged us inside, and I swatted Mitch's hand away when he put it on my lower back.

"Hi, I'm Riley," my little sister greeted Mitch the second he walked through the door. "I'm Jamie's younger, very mature sister." The way Mitch tried to hide his discomfort at Riley's attempt to flirt with him made me crack a smile.

"She still sleeps with her dolls," Trevor added. Riley punched him in the arm, giving him a death glare.

"She's definitely your little sister," Mitch whispered against the shell of my ear. The feel of his lips sent a slight tremor through my body, but I quickly squashed it by elbowing him in the side. He chuckled, which only pissed me off more.

"I'm, Ryan, Jamie's father." My dad was a huge man who scared the crap out of almost everyone. Mitch only gave him a smile and offered his hand to shake. I couldn't help but notice Mitch's shoulders were just as broad as my fathers.

"Nice to meet you. I've heard a lot about you," Mitch added. My brows furrowed in his direction. He didn't know that much about my family; we'd only talked about them once.

"Funny, we've never heard of you." My mother gave me an irritated glance, but I ignored her as she took Mitch's arm into the kitchen to give him a plate of food. "Wow, you've got some big muscles!" she added as she led him through the door frame. Both my father and I rolled our eyes simultaneously.

"Watch out, Jamie. Mom's going to make a move on your boyfriend," Trevor said while helping the twins with their helicopters.

"He's not my boyfriend," I scolded while pushing his hat down further on his head.

"He's not?" Riley said with hope.

"No, and he's not interested in teenage girls either," my father added before I had the chance.

"We were just about to play cards," my mother announced as she came back into the living room with Mitch. He was carrying a plate full of food. He sat down at the table and crooked his finger for me to come and sit by him, but I shook my head. He needed to know following me to my parent's house was not cool, and not safe for all parties involved.

"Do you play Seven Up, Mitch?" my mother asked, sitting across from him with a few decks in hand.

"No, but I'd love to learn."

"I'm not sure you could handle it," I said coldly to Mitch.

"If the twins can play, I'm sure he can figure it out. Come on kids, Ryan, let's play," my mother insisted while shuffling the cards. My little brothers groaned, but Riley jumped from her seat on the couch, rushing to sit next to Mitch. I chuckled, loving how Mitch shied away from her.

"Riley, you need to sit by the twins and help them," my father scolded, forcing her to move so he could sit by Mitch. The old sheriff in him was coming out, and that made me smile even more.

"Jamie, come on. Don't keep your guest waiting," my mother urged. Reluctantly, I sat on the other side of Mitch.

He leaned into my side, coming close to my ear. "I'm offended you don't think I can handle Seven Up."

"It's numbers," I mumbled.

"Low blow," he grumbled back playfully. "Besides, I can count the shapes."

I huffed while sitting back further in my chair and crossing my arms.

***

"Jamie, are you sure you and Mitch have to leave? Trevor can stay with the twins tonight and the two of you can have his room," my mother begged as I pushed Mitch out the door. We played cards for nearly two hours, then Mitch played video games with my little brothers for another two.

"We'd need two rooms, and no, we both have to work in the morning," I grumbled.

"You *would* need two rooms," my father interjected in agreement. But then, to my surprise, he smacked Mitch on the back, giving him a wink. Mitch smirked back, and I almost blew a gasket.

"Thank you for the hospitality," Mitch said politely, reaching both arms out to give my mother a hug.

"Stop glaring, Jamie. It's not polite," she scolded over Mitch's shoulder as she hugged him back. I rolled my eyes, causing her to grumble under her breath in disapproval.

"I'll call you both later, goodnight," I said in a rush as I power-walked to my car.

Mitch waved one final goodbye to my parents then followed me to my car. "Can we talk?"

"I have nothing to say to you."

"Why are you so pissed off?" he asked irritably, moving his hand to block me from opening my door.

"Because you followed me to my parents house and acted like we're a couple!"

His arms crossed as he leaned against my door, now making it impossible for me to open it. I threw my hands in the air in defeat.

"We aren't together!"

Mitch cocked his head. "Last night's actions might beg to differ with that statement."

I narrowed my eyes at him. "We were drunk. And I thought you could handle a one night stand."

"We weren't drunk this morning."

My eyes met the ground as I bit my lip, remembering how perfect this morning felt. I wanted him, more than anything, but risking the safety of the ones I loved wasn't worth it.

Mitch uncrossed his arms and reached to hold my hands. They were nearly twice the size of mine. He stepped in front of me, tipping his head low, trying to get me to look up at him. "Jamie, I know someone hurt you, and these feelings are hard to accept, but baby, we were meant for each other."

The lump that was forming in my throat was thicker than it had been in a long time. I believed his every word, but he didn't understand.

"Look. Let's start over. I know you need to gain my trust. We can go slow." His thumbs brushed rhythmically against the tops of my hands as he spoke. "We can fight, flirt, act like we hate each other all we want, but this," he pulled my hand to his heart, "this wants every single piece of you. Please, let me prove it."

"Slow?" My voice cracked, knowing this was going to be the only way I'd get him out of my parents' street and far away from any danger.

He nodded, letting go of my hand so he could cradle my face. "Like molasses." A small smile crept across my lips, causing his grin to widen. "Can I have a kiss to tide me over for whenever you decide the time is right again?"

I rolled my eyes, but held my smile as his thumb traced my cheek bone. "And I thought you were supposed to be aggressive."

He shook his head while laughing, then leaned in for a kiss that was surprisingly tender and sweet. My body was awakened, but I firmly held my hands to my sides, not wanting to let the evening go any further than it already had.

Mitch pulled away, licking his lips as our foreheads met. "Can I have one more night?"

"Mitch…" I wanted many more nights, but it couldn't happen.

"I know, I know. Slow… You're more than worth the wait, Jamie Rae."

Tears threatened as I wrapped my arms around his waist. Fighting these feelings was going to be the hardest battle I'd had my entire life.

CHAPTER FOUR

Jamie, age 18.

The past six months I'd been on autopilot.

I'd turned eighteen and was in my final month of high school. I still had no life, and my house was tense because my father had lost his job. He couldn't be in any police department in the state, so was forced to find a factory job that paid half as much as his previous salary.

The uncontrollable guilt was consuming me. The same day I'd planned to confront Rod, my father stormed out of his workplace saying he'd resigned because of upper management. He was calm and collected when he talked to my mother about it, reassuring her everything would be fine and that they'd be okay. The pit in my stomach grew knowing it was because of me that he'd quit, and he hadn't looked me in the eye since that day. My poor decisions were a constant kick in the ass.

But there were two good things: I wasn't pregnant with Rod's demon child like I had feared, and Rod hadn't contacted me. My heart played tricks on me, though. As afraid of Rod as I was, I partially missed him. He wasn't always a monster, passionate and kind at points in our relationship. He'd taken so much from me, yet I still remembered the few good things he introduced me to. Admitting I loved him was painful, and I hated that some nights I'd still daydream about the few moments where he was tender.

Landon was my saving grace. He knew my secret and miraculously hadn't share it with anyone in our family. But since he'd finished his first semester of college and left for basic training, I'd tortured myself with silence. I missed him terribly, but the contact we could have was slim since he had to focus on his training. I was proud of him, but I was dying inside.

"Jamie, are you sure you don't want to go to your senior prom?" my mother asked as she sat down on the couch next to me.

I shook my head. "I'm fine, Mom. Besides, it's expensive and overly done. Who actually remembers their high school prom?"

"I do, sweetheart."

My lip quirked. I wasn't sure, but from mine and Landon's calculations, he was conceived in May of our parents' senior year of high school. Not that we really wanted to think of that day.

"It's fine. Besides, Landon will be home. I'd rather spend the time with him," I said truthfully, warmth filling me knowing I'd see him within a week's time.

"Yes, we should plan a get together and invite all the family. Want to help?"

I nodded, grateful for the distraction.

***

"The signs at the airport were a bit much, Mom." Landon blushed as he walked into our new home. We'd moved into a smaller house while he was away because of my father's job change, another reason for the knife to twist further into my gut.

I nudged his side with my elbow. "We were the ones who needed the signs. You look so different." He was broader in the shoulders, more muscular, and his hair was buzzed short underneath his side cap. He stood tall and proud in his Air Force uniform that he'd worked hard to earn.

He grinned. "Now the ladies really won't be able to keep their eyes off me."

My entire family laughed as we entered our home. After a large family meal my mother prepared, we went about our normal Saturday routine. It felt good to have him home. Our family wasn't complete without Landon.

I found my way to the porch swing I'd grown accustomed to sitting on by myself the last few months. The gentle creaking sound it made with a steady swing was soothing along with the birds rummaging in the pine trees.

Landon noticed me staring off into the smaller backyard. He took a seat next to me, following my gaze. "So … this weekend … I hear it's prom."

I let out a soft breath. "Yeah, should be a banging time."

"So you're going?"

I laughed. "Not a chance in hell."

He laughed with me. "What if you had the most charming date on your arm?"

I raised a brow. "I haven't been in the mood for a date."

Landon rested his elbows on his knees. "Mom and Dad said you've been off. Have you told them?"

My voice was barely a whisper. "I can't."

"They aren't going to let you go to FSU in the fall if you don't start acting normal."

"What?" FSU was my only hope for my life to maybe go back to normal. A new place where I'd be on my own and able to focus on my future. A place that would be hours away from Rod.

"I bet, if you took your older brother to prom, they'd think you were just missing me."

"I have nothing to wear, no tickets, and the prom starts in four hours. I wouldn't even know what to do with my hair."

"I could help with hair," my mother suddenly said from the porch. I turned to look, seeing her standing there with my father. "You could take the Grand Prix. Not too fancy, but nicer than the Corolla."

"Mom got a dress for you, too!" Riley piped in, more excited than anyone else here. She was already more girly than I was.

Landon stood then reached his hand out to me. "So, what do you say? Will you go to prom with me?"

"All right," I conceded as though I were being forced to go to my senior prom, but I was excited.

***

"Red looks great with my uniform, don't you think?" Landon brushed his uniform with his palms, more looking at himself in the review mirror than at my red strapless dress. It went perfectly with my beauty queen curls and red heels.

"We are quite patriotic," I sighed.

He turned to me and smiled, his aviators covering his eyes. "Dinner was great, now on to the dance. Honestly, I think I stayed for only ten minutes of my prom."

"That's because you and Kevin went to go smoke pot and drink at an after party."

His lip twitched. "Yeah, we did. Look, we'll get the prom photo, have some spiked punch, dance to a few songs, then head to a party. Sound good?"

I stared down at the silver sparkly nail polish Riley painted on my nails while my mother curled my caramel hair. "I don't know." I mainly didn't know because I had no idea where a party would be.

"A friend of mine is throwing a party. Would that be cool enough for an after-prom shin dig?" Landon asked while pulling into the dance.

I'd only drank with Landon and his friends a few times. Maybe getting drunk would help me to relax a little. As long as none of his friends hit on me, especially Kevin.

Reading my mind again, he added, "I promise Kevin will be on his best behavior."

"Okay. Can we just go to his house?"

"No, I promised Mom we'd get a picture."

I groaned in annoyance, causing Landon to laugh. "A half hour tops, I promise."

That half hour couldn't have gone any slower. I don't think any of the kids noticed who I was. Even Bethany didn't say hi to me. She looked wonderful and I smiled at her, but she only turned up her nose and kept walking. Every other girl who walked by us giggled and blushed at Landon. They all knew him. He was known as the stud a grade ahead of us. He would wink at them and smile, flirt a little when a few of them had the courage to talk to him. They ignored me every time.

"Can we go yet?" I whined.

"After we dance. Come on." He motioned to the dance floor as the lights went lower, the disco ball turning in beat with the slow song. I rolled my eyes, feeling like an official loser for dancing at my high school prom with my older brother. Reluctantly, I took his hand, and we went into a formal step together.

"This is awkward. They're all staring at you," I muttered.

"No way, all the guys in here haven't taken their greedy little eyes off you," Landon countered as we swayed to the music. I dipped my head low, not wanting to believe him. "They're staring at you because they don't recognize you. You've changed this past year. You're more grown up, stronger. I know you don't feel that way because of that fucker Rod, but I see it, Jamie. Most girls wouldn't have pushed that dip shit away like you did."

"I should have done it sooner," I whispered quietly.

"Maybe so, but you did it. Ninety percent of women would still be taking orders and beatings from that asshole. Not you, Jamie. You've beaten the odds."

My chin found his shoulder as my stomach fell. "Then why do I still think about him? Why at night when I'm lonely do I remember all the good in him?"

Landon stared down at me, pity in his eyes. "You thought you loved him, Jay. He fed you lies, and you were young and naïve, but not anymore."

I nodded, believing him. I was stronger than that asshole.

"Has he tried to contact you at all?"

I shook my head.

"Good. Try to forget about him, okay?"

"That's the ultimate goal."

***

"Kevin's got a new place with some roommates from college. He says it's really nice," Landon said with excitement. He hadn't seen any of his friends yet, and I could tell by the extra skip to his jump that he was eager to throw back a drink with his buddies.

I smiled and followed him. "We should have brought different clothes," I said, feeling out of place as we approached the front porch filled with people in jeans and T-shirts.

"Who cares?" Landon said, opening the door.

"Look who it is! My airman!" Kevin hollered, jumping out of his seat while holding a beer in each hand. "Look how official you are, suit and all. Way to outdo us all, you bastard!" Landon's smile was wide as he greeted his friends. I stumbled behind, feeling like an idiot.

"Jamie, you look hot as hell!" Kevin whistled, putting his arm around me. "Damn it, why didn't things work out between us?"

"Because you're a fucking moron," Landon shouted past us. I noticed he already had his arm around a girl who looked familiar. If I didn't know any better, I'd say it was the girl he took to his own prom.

"Jamie, come on, let's catch up. I've missed you the past few months while ole' Lando here has been away at camp," Kevin said with a pout. I couldn't help but smile at him. He was always nice to me and acted like a brother most of the time. I felt safe with him at least, and that was something rare after Rod.

We all started playing drinking games. I hadn't had a lot, but could hold my liquor very well, and I wasn't even feeling buzzed after the first few rounds of flip cup. Landon wandered off once we began beer pong. Kevin was my partner, and we'd won five games in a row, which meant the drinking hadn't been as heavy for us.

Kevin took a swig of his beer, then called for a break. "Come on, Jay. Let me give you a graduation present." I stopped in my tracks, worried what might happen. He stopped and turned, giving me a puzzled look. "Come on, I'm not going to try anything stupid. Your brother just doubled his weight in muscle, and even though he's probably deep in that blonde's tits right now, he'd still pull out to come kick my ass."

I winced at the picture that formed in my head as I followed Kevin onto the front porch. It wasn't crowded anymore because everyone had moved to the backyard for the bonfire.

We took a seat on the steps. Kevin pulled out a lighter and a zip lock bag from his pants pocket that contained a joint. Handing me the bag, he smiled. "Happy graduation."

Taking the bag, I returned his smile. "Um, thanks?"

"You need to have a little fun, and a joint will loosen you up. I've seen what you're like with a good amount of booze in you. Let's party it up!"

"Yeah, but I've never smoked before. I could be a complete bitch for all you know."

"You already are," he teased, elbowing me in the bicep. I laughed, then pulled the joint from the bag. Kevin took out his Zippo and helped me to light the joint, taking a puff first himself. He passed it over, giving me a wink.

Why the hell not? Maybe it would temporarily erase all of my mistakes. I took a hit, trying not to cough as the smoke infiltrated my lungs.

Kevin laughed as I covered my mouth. "You took that like a champ. Most girls puke." Taking another puff, I relaxed more, leaning my back on the railing. This wasn't bad at all. We passed the joint back and forth until it was gone, then stared off into the dark space. Kevin would ramble, but I merely stared, not thinking about anything. People were coming and going, but we only sat, mellow and calm.

The voice that came from behind me sent chills up and down my back, pulling me from my high. "Jamie? Is that you?" Rod's frame was taking up the threshold of the door, some chick was on his side, kissing on his neck while her hand wandered into the front of his pants. He shoved her aside when he saw me, his eyes becoming larger with each step.

"What the fuck?" he said in confusion, staring at Kevin's arm that was now draped around my shoulders. I hadn't even noticed Kevin was touching me. Before I knew what was happening, Rod ripped Kevin's arm from my shoulders, shoving him down the few steps from the porch.

"Dude?" Kevin shouted as he stumbled to his feet.

"Get away from my girl," Rod demanded as he stood in front of me protectively. I backed away instinctively, not sure what was going on.

"Since when? Dude, she's like a little sister to me. I mean, don't get me wrong—she's hot as shit. And if she gave me a chance I'd probably go for it, but come on," Kevin rambled as he dusted off his jeans.

Rod turned to face me, sadness filling his eyes. "Can we talk? I miss you, Jamie."

I swallowed hard, not sure what to say to him. He'd lost weight, his face thinner than when I'd stroke the stubble on his jaw. His hair was longer now, curling past his ears. I remembered when I'd tug on it as he made love to me. I also remembered when I'd pull on it wanting him to stop choking me, so I shook my head no.

Rod's eyes grew wide. "Are you really with this stoner?"

"No, I just don't want to talk to you."

Rod stormed down the stairs until he was directly in front of me, his scent fresh in my nostrils, a smell that used to turn me on, but now brought on fear. "You listen—"

"I thought I told you to stay the fuck away from my sister," Landon growled from the entrance to the house. The blonde he was with earlier nowhere in sight. His muscles looked huge in his button up uniform, and anyone who tried to mess with him was surely an idiot.

Rod looked into my eyes but slowly turned to face Landon. "I thought you were off being the best you could be?"

Landon walked down the steps until he was toe to toe with Rod. Last time I was worried about Landon, but this time Rod was the one who'd be in trouble.

"No, I aim high, fly-fight-win, you dip shit. You lay a finger on her and I'll break your neck," Landon snarled.

"Aren't you precious in your little uniform. Too bad daddy lost his."

Rod was egging Landon on, and it wasn't going to be good. He'd been drinking, and the way his eyes were bloodshot wasn't a good sign.

"Gentleman, let's cool down," Kevin said, moving his hands between the two men. "This is a celebration, after all. Landon's home, Jamie's prom, come on, can't we all get along?"

Rod turned to look at me. "Let's go talk. I've changed, Jamie."

Landon reached for Rod's shoulder, turning him so he was facing him again. "Don't even look at her. She wants nothing to do with you."

Rod's lip curled. "She wanted me. I couldn't keep her off my dick."

Landon lost it, winding his arm back and making a hard blow to Rod's right eye, causing him to go tumbling down. Kevin backed away toward me while Landon continued to beat him with reckless abandonment.

"Landon, stop!" I shouted, Kevin holding me back. "You'll get into trouble!"

Just as Landon looked toward me, Rod caught him off guard, throwing a punch to his gut, bringing Landon to his knees. Rod stumbled up, knocking his fist into the side of Landon's head.

"Stop it!" I screamed again. "Please! You're hurting each other!"

The devil was in Rod's eyes as he kept punching, relentless blows while Landon tried to stand and defend himself. A crowd was forming now, and I was furious no one was trying to stop them. Just as Rod was going to throw another punch at Landon, Landon leaped toward Rod's knees, causing him to tumble to his back. Now Landon was straddling him, sending hit after hit to Rod's face. He was bleeding from his nose and lips, bruises already forming on his face.

I wailed and begged for them to stop, sick of the fighting and the anger in both their eyes. Finally, Landon stood, straightening his shirt and rubbing the blood from his mouth with his hand. "Stay the fuck away from her," he threatened one last time while his chest heaved.

"Let's go," I said firmly to Landon, reaching for his arm and yanking it toward the car.

"I can't fucking drive," Landon said as he stumbled alongside me.

"I'm fine. We need to get out of here. That was amazingly stupid of you to do," I chided Landon as we got to the car. "Do you know who his grandfather is? He's the head of all the police in Florida. Probably the reason why Dad can't get a job anywhere else!"

"Fuck," Landon mumbled, wiping his nose again. I handed him a sweatshirt from the backseat.

"This whole night was a mistake," I muttered into the steering wheel as I pulled out of Kevin's street.

"Whatever, that sick bastard had it coming to him."

"I just hope it doesn't get you into trouble," I sighed, realizing this fight could jeopardize everything Landon had worked so hard for the past few months.

He shook his head, acting invincible, then we both jolted forward in our seats.

BAM!

A car bumped us from behind, then did it again.

BAM!

The strong force caused us both to lurch forward, my chest burning from the seatbelt. "What the hell?" I shrieked, trying to gain control of the steering wheel so we wouldn't fly off the road and into the trees.

Landon flung his head toward the back, trying to look out the window, but all he could see were headlights. *BAM*, another blow, but now the car sped up to the side, roaring so he was even with us in the other lane. It was Rod, murder in his eyes as he looked at the two of us from the window. He mouthed for me to pull over, but there was no way I'd stop the car for that sick and twisted man. Especially with the insanity in his eyes. I'd seen the damage he could do in that state of mind.

"Go faster!" Landon ordered, wanting to get away from the sick freak as bad as I did, but Rod was keeping the same pace, no matter how heavy I laid on the gas pedal. The car began to shake with the speed, and the steering wheel fought me as I hit the gravel. Rod was slowly pushing me off the side of the road with his car, getting pushed until half the car was completely off the road. The trees were getting closer and closer with every inch Rod pushed.

Tears of fear sprung from my eyes, wanting more than anything to not be in control of the car. "Focus, Jay. You can do this," Landon encouraged, although I could sense the tension in his voice.

My instincts kicked in, focusing on Newton's laws of motion. I slammed on my brakes, hoping to stay at rest, but my tires skidded in the gravel, my back end swinging into a complete circle. We bounced, nearly rolling to one side, but thankfully fell back on all fours and right up against a tree trunk. I shrieked as my side of the car dented inward, touching my thighs, my breath halting as the car finally stilled.

"You all right?" Landon asked, reaching over to touch my arm. I nodded, my body shaking from the adrenaline of our crash. With trembling hands, I attempted to maneuver away from the tree, but it was pointless. The car was jammed and the steering wheel wouldn't turn. We were trapped now, at Rod's mercy.

My heart pounded as I saw the headlights shining in Landon's direction. Landon hadn't noticed because he was too focused on making sure I was okay. My eyes widened in horror as the sound of his engine revved, then the screeching of his tires blared through the dark of the night.

"No!" I screamed as one final blow hit us. Glass shattered, bending the metal of the car with a loud creak. Landon howled along with the sound of metal crunching, but it wasn't metal, it was his legs. Landon was pinned from the waist down, his body warped where his head was in my lap.

"Landon!" I screamed.

My hands reached to try and pull him, but it only caused a blood-curdling scream to come from his mouth. He was trapped between pieces of the car, smashed together like a metal sandwich. I thrashed inside the car, attempting to wiggle my way out in every way possible to find help. I shouted at the top of my lungs, begging for a sign of life to come and rescue us, but it was no use. It was one o'clock in the morning on a nearly deserted road. My head slammed backward into the headrest, my fists pounding against the steering wheel. Landon moaned, and I moved my hands to cradle his face.

"Someone will come soon, Landon. You'll be okay," I assured him soothingly.

***

The hours passed as I listened to the calmness of the night mingling with Landon's whimpers. My legs were cramped and numb from the lack of blood flow. My back ached, and the headlights from Rod's car had finally disappeared, leaving us in the moonlight. I was running out of ways to distract us from the terrible situation we were trapped in.

"Soon, you'll be doped up on pain meds, and I'll make sure the most attractive nurse will be by your bedside at your beck and call."

He let out a slight laugh, followed by a groan. I winced as I helplessly watched, running my fingers over his eyebrows and along the buzzed cut of his hair. It was something my mother always did when I had a bad dream. The way his face slightly relaxed led me to believe my mother did the same for him.

His heavily lidded brown eyes met mine. I bit my lip to stop it from trembling, but my voice shook with uncertainty. "You're going to be okay." I wanted to sound brave and convincing, but the light was fading from his eyes as his shallow breaths began to slow. "Hang in there with me, Landon. Please. I can't lose you." Tears flowed from my eyes like an endless faucet. He was my everything, the only person who'd made me smile in months and understood why I was the way I was. He was practically my twin, only separated by eleven months. Landon had always been the strong one, and my weakness was overpowering me. I couldn't let him go.

He gurgled before he barely whispered the words, "You're the fighter, Jay." He gulped, closing his eyes briefly, and when he opened them again, the pain that was written on his face evaporated as though he saw the light at the end of the tunnel, taking him from this world.

"No," I said sternly. "Don't you dare leave me!" I shook his head firmly in my hands, pleading with him not to give in to the other side.

His lips parted slightly. "Fight... for me..." He faded, his eyes drifting away from mine, staring as though he was looking right through me. After another gurgle, blood began to pour from his mouth and drain from his ears as his body spasmed to fight for his life. He was trapped and bleeding from the inside out, and all I could do was yell for help.

Utter, painful wails beseeching for hope.

CHAPTER FIVE

Keeping Mitch at arm's length wasn't a walk in the park. Not because he wasn't giving me my space, but because I couldn't stop thinking about him. Every time the door to the office would open, my head would whip up, hoping to see his smug grin walking through the door, white T-shirt and jeans looking sexy as ever. But I was repeatedly let down. I'd hardly talked to him, besides the daily pick-up line texts that I looked forward to.

Mitch: I want to live in your socks so I can be with you every step of the way.

My phone rang, saving me from my sorrowful thoughts. "Hello?" I answered without looking at the screen.

"So is there any room in your socks for me?"

My grin was wide as my breath caught.

"My feet are pretty small."

"Hmm… I guess I could squeeze into your bra, although you fill that sucker up nicely."

I leaned back in my chair, thankful no one could see my blush. "You're such a boob guy."

"Mmm, yes I am. Only yours, though." I sighed heavily, feeling my heart thump loudly as I closed my eyes. "Sorry, that wasn't very appropriate," he corrected.

"No, it wasn't. Where are you?" I asked, wanting to change the subject.

"I'm in Chicago, have been for a week now. We've been finishing up a new high-rise. Thankfully, I'll be in Grand Rapids all next week." He paused for a moment. "Are you going to be at Becca and Tyler's welcome home party from their honeymoon?"

I'd been looking forward to that party for the past three weeks. I'd missed Becca and the Conklin's, especially Mitch. Trying to hide the excitement in my voice I replied, "Yes, my flight leaves Saturday morning. I'll be staying in Grand Rapids the following week as well."

"Yeah? Maybe we could grab coffee or dinner?"

"Maybe." Keeping him at a distance was going to be difficult while we were in the same city.

He sighed into the phone. "We'll talk at Tyler and Becca's?"

"Of course."

***

My stomach was in knots and I'd even puked a few times, worried sick about seeing Mitch and not being able to keep my distance.

Nathan and I rode together from my condo in Grand Rapids to Becca and Tyler's house in Grand Haven. It was great catching up with Nathan as we went, but I couldn't help daydreaming about Mitch and our night under the stars.

I thought about how I'd greet Mitch. Would I hug him? Wave? Ignore him until he approached me? I was putting way too much thought into seeing Mitch when today wasn't even about him. I wanted to hear all about Becca's honeymoon. She greeted me from the front porch of her beautiful lakeside home. It was her dream floor plan, and I was happy Tyler could make her dreams come true. She was glowing as we hugged, the smile on her face giddy. She hugged Nathan quickly after me, then latched her arm with mine.

"Good trip?" I asked, kissing her cheek.

"Jamie, it was amazing."

"I can't wait to hear all about it," I said enthusiastically as we walked inside.

"Well, not too much," Nathan teased as Tyler met us halfway.

"I don't kiss and tell," Tyler laughed, holding his hands to his sides. I snickered inwardly, knowing Becca would tell me everything.

We greeted Becca's family, along with Nathan and Tyler's mom as we entered. The only person missing was Mitch, and my stomach was churning. Was he not going to show up because I'd been so wishy-washy on the phone with him?

"Let's eat before it gets cold! Mitch texted me saying he was running behind and to start without him," Mary said. My face remained neutral, but my heart fluttered. Mitch was going to be here, and I couldn't want to see him.

Brunch was lovely. It was strange seeing Becca so chipper and chatty. She normally sat back and listened, but was beyond thrilled to discuss all the sites and activities they'd done while on the honeymoon of their dreams.

We'd cleared the table and gathered around the living room to watch Becca and Tyler open wedding gifts when Mitch briskly walked inside, waving both hands in greeting. Becca jumped up to give him a hug, along with Tyler and his mother. Once we were settled, Mitch meandered to the kitchen in search of food.

"I'm going to get a mimosa, want one?" I asked Nathan. He studied me, then shook his head, continuing to watch Becca and Tyler open their gifts. As nonchalantly as I could, I made my way to the fridge, grabbing the orange juice and champagne.

"Hey, stranger," Mitch said subtly while loading up his plate.

"Hi," I whispered while moving closer to him to grab a flute from a cupboard above the sink. He was inches away now, and I couldn't help but smell his woodsy scent. His arm touched my lower back as I stood on my tip toes.

"I could have gotten that for you," he murmured close to my ear as I stretched. My body stilled for a moment, enjoying our closeness.

"It's fine," I said quickly, taking a step back from him, aware of our company. I caught the grin on his face out of the corner of my eye. Fixing my drink, I found my place back by Nathan on the couch. He was smirking at me as I sat down.

"How's your drink?" he asked with a smug smile.

I nudged his bicep for teasing me.

***

"Jamie, I need to look at a property out this way. Do you mind?" Nathan asked as we began to say our goodbyes. I really didn't feel like working, but the expression on Nathan's face meant it wasn't an option to say no.

"I'll take you back. I'm heading to Grand Rapids," Mitch offered.

"You don't have to do that," I said instinctively, although every bone in my body wanted to drive with him for hours upon hours, escaping far away from my demons.

"I know, but I want to."

"I'd go with Mitch," Becca said with a knowing smile. She didn't know Mitch and I had spent the night together after her wedding, but I thought she had an inkling something had happened between us.

"Who knows how long I'll take," Nathan added while looking at his phone.

"Okay." My voice was quiet, but my body shivered as Mitch led me out the door and to his car. To my surprise, he didn't have his car. He walked toward a black motorcycle. "What is that?"

Mitch grinned, walking toward it to grab one of the helmets to hand to me. "It's my baby."

"I'm not riding on that."

"Come on, Jay. I thought you liked the fast lane?" Shoving the helmet in my hands, he added, "Please, I've been dreaming about you behind me on this bike for God knows how long."

My heart fluttered at his words, my eyes hypnotized by the sparkle in his green eyes. I huffed, wanting to look reluctant as I put the helmet on, and Mitch gave me a megawatt smile in return. He was beginning to be able to see past my mask, and I wasn't sure how I felt about that.

"Good thing you wore jeans and that leather jacket," he winked, climbing onto the bike. Finding my courage, I straddled the bike behind him and wrapped my arms around his waist. "This is the real reason I brought the bike," he flirted.

I shook my head and smacked his shoulder, causing him to chuckle. He started it up, revving the engine and causing it to roar to life. My breath caught in my throat as he darted down the curved driveway. He zipped and zoomed around cars on the highway, and I squeezed him tighter each time he weaved.

He'd tease me through the headsets in the helmets when I'd get anxious, and I'd curse and shout back at him. It only fueled him to tease me more. Our relationship was strange, but comforting.

When we reached Grand Rapids, Mitch didn't take me to my condo, but instead back to the high rises he'd been working on. They looked beautiful. I couldn't help but think back to the night we'd stargazed at the top and how he'd held me all night.

"Want to come up and see? My suite is finished," Mitch said with excitement. "This is where I've really been the past few weeks, not Chicago. If you'd wondered at all."

I had wondered, and it made sense. Mitch helped me climb off his bike, never letting go of my hand. No one was in the building, which gave me time to appreciate the marble floors and high ceilings of the main lobby; it had been dark and unfinished the last time we were here together. Mitch pulled a key card from his pocket, swiping it over the pad next to the elevator.

"This is turning out great, Mitch," I complimented.

"Yeah, I think once Kobiashi's amusement park is done, I might stay here more often."

My heart twisted. I wanted to be in Grand Rapids again too, not Florida. "I can't wait to see your place."

The doors opened directly to his unit. The floors were in now, beautiful dark hardwood spread throughout the wide space, and dark accents trimmed the white walls. His furniture was sparse, but I'd assumed he just hadn't had time to make the place his. Making our way to his bedroom, I was surprised by just how little there was. A bed sat in the middle with one dresser on the side holding an alarm clock and a lamp.

"Needs a woman's touch," he said softly.

His hand found my lower back, trailing up my spine and to the neck of my jacket. I gulped, unsure if I could fight my heart any longer. Both his hands were on me now, slowly helping to remove my jacket from behind. His breath was heavy as we stared at his bed. Both our minds in the same place, but terrified to make the move.

"I've missed you," he murmured across my neck, one hand running down my hip while the other worked at my ponytail. His lips were so close, begging to taste me, but he wouldn't do it without my permission. I turned to face him, my eyes heavy with indecision.

"What's holding you back?" he asked softly, his hand tracing my jaw.

"I don't want you to get hurt," I whispered. It was the truth.

"Then don't break my heart. I'm going to kiss you," he breathed across my cheek. My eyes fluttered shut, waiting for the moment I'd longed for the past month. My conscience screamed at me, but I was going to be selfish tonight. After all, Rod hadn't shown his face or written any cryptic letters since the night after the wedding.

His lips touched the side of my mouth, asking for permission. The moment I felt the contact, I gasped, reaching my hands around his shoulders and diving in, kissing him like I needed it to breath.

Mitch groaned into my mouth, dipping his tongue with mine as his arms held me close to his chest. He swiftly lifted my legs to wrap around his waist, walking us until we were aligned with the bed. I pulled back from the kiss long enough to look into his lust-filled eyes.

"I'm not sure if I can go slow tonight," he rasped, licking his lips.

"So don't," I coaxed, pulling his face back to mine.

Unhooking my ankles from his waist, he set me down so I was sitting on the edge of the bed. I reached for my shirt, lifting it over my head and tossing it on the floor. Mitch's eyes widened when they found my lacy red bra, pushing my girls to their fullest.

"Yep, not going to be able to go slow," he said rapidly, falling to his knees in front of me.

His mouth found the top of my breasts in a rush, heavily panting between each suck. I giggled, my hands grabbing the back of his head. He nuzzled between them, his arms locking around my lower back. Frenzied, open-mouthed kisses ran across my skin, making its way to my collarbone, causing my giggles to turn into gasps. My head tipped back, relishing the feeling of his need to consume me.

My heart pounded as he made his way toward the base of my neck, mentally telling myself he was kissing me there because it made me feel good and not because he wanted to drain the life from my eyes. As though he were reading my thoughts, his mouth moved slower, taking its time as it traveled upward. His soft lips mended my scars with each gentle suck.

My body went lax, accepting his devotion. I gripped his strong shoulders, enjoying how they were flexed and taut under the pads of my fingers. I sighed as he found my jaw, working his way back to my lips. His grip loosened around me, moving to my waist and pushing me backward so I was lying flat on my back.

Rising from his knees, his hand ran down my stomach, stopping at the button on my jeans. I smirked at him, urging him to undo it. Meeting my grin, he swiftly opening the button with one hand, then tugged my jeans off my legs, tossing them to the floor. The low growl that erupted from his chest was primitive. Maybe he loved the matching red lace thong.

My chest rose as I arched my back, feeling seductive and powerful.

I slowly opened my legs, inviting him to have his way with me. That mouth was more than welcome to repeat the passionate movements from earlier. A devious grin crossed his face as he watched my actions.

"Want something in particular?"

My hand caressed down my belly and to my pubic bone. Lust filled eyes followed intently, his lip firmly between his teeth in anticipation of where it was headed. "Let me point you in the right direction," I said slyly. My clit was sensitive as my thumb brushed over the top of the red lace. I moaned slightly, arching my back in pleasure.

Mitch took my hand. "I think I get it," he said huskily as he lowered to his knees, yanking the scraps of red lace down my legs. Those open mouthed kisses I loved so much found the insides of my thighs, causing goose bumps to form on my skin. The ache in my core throbbed the closer his teasing lips came to my sensitive folds and I groaned in frustration, wanting him to make a meal of me.

"Is someone getting impatient?" he teased, blowing his warm breath across my sex. My hips pressed upward, demanding to be touched. "I'm just giving you some well-needed attention between your legs."

I sat up, my hand curling around the back of his neck. "Don't make me get off in front of you and then put my clothes on and walk out that door."

The ear to ear grin on Mitch's face pissed me off so much that I began to sit up, but hands gripped my hips, forcing me back down.

"I don't fucking think so."

Just as I was going to give him hell, his hands shoved my thighs apart, mouth meeting my skin with desperate need. He moved fast, flicking his tongue as though it was a boxer working a speed bag.

"Holy shit," I gasped at the rise in my pulse.

His mouth moved over my sensitive nub, working like a suction cup now. I ground my hips upward, urging him to suck harder. The need to come from his mouth was overwhelming. I wanted him to fill me, lick me, suck me, everything all at once.

"Yes," I encouraged, moving my hips faster with the rhythm of his tongue, circling and flicking in perfect unison.

One last flick, and I was in oblivion, my hips bucking wildly into him as he nuzzled my sex, sucking hard as my clit throbbed in his mouth. Mitch's groan of pleasure mumbled through my skin, causing my orgasm to tingle throughout my whole body.

His head popped up, watching me as I came down from my high. Once my eyes met his, a finger slowly worked through my folds, stretching me as my muscles pulsed. Mitch's eyes rolled as he sunk another finger inside, working them steadily in and out.

"This is so fucking hot," he breathed, his eyes moving between mine and the way he was working his fingers inside of me. I began to sit up so I could watch his fingers move from a better angle but was pushed down by his other hand. "I'm not done with you yet."

My insides clenched around his fingers again at his words, hoping he'd never be through with working me over. A rumble came from his chest as he removed his fingers, crawling slowly onto the bed so he was lying next to me. His hand slid across my stomach in preparation to attack.

"Your tits look amazing right now. Begging me to yank them out of that lace and suck them," he growled as his hands moved to cup one heavy breast.

I groaned in satisfaction as his hand dipped under the fabric, revealing my nipple for his mouth to devour. Tremors rumbled to my core as he repeated the same pleasurable movement with his tongue, flicking and sucking until the urge to burst overcame me. His arm reached under my arched back, unclasping the strap to completely reveal my breasts.

"Fuck me," he groaned, burrowing his head between them.

I couldn't take it anymore. My hands found his chest, firmly beginning to push him on his back, but he resisted, his arms caging me as his body went to hover over mine. My breath hitched as his hips wedged their way between my legs, his cock laying heavy on my stomach. I'd never allowed myself to be put in this position, a man able to have the upper hand. The times when a man surrounded me like this, I'd end up not being able to breath.

"You ready for me?" he asked, resting his elbows on either side of my head.

I pushed my need to control away and nodded.

I trusted him.

He moved his hips slowly, rubbing the tip of his cock between my lips, brushing my clit in the process causing me to wince slightly. I was still sensitive from the way his mouth worked me moments ago but craved another round.

He bit his lip while looking down at me, passion and lust filling his green eyes. "Tell me if you need me to stop. Because I will, Jay. I don't want to hurt you."

My heart fluttered, reaching my hand to stroke his cheek as he looked down at me affectionately. He wasn't being cocky about his size, something I'd have assumed before I'd gotten to know him. He was worried about my past, unsure exactly where my pain had bled from. But he was good at reading between the lines, picking up on small quirks that got to me. He had the ability—the *devotion* to look deep into the depths of my soul, willing to protect me from my darkest demons.

He was healing me.

Let me take it away, Jamie.

"Okay," I spoke softly.

He lowered his head down so our foreheads were touching. My other hand found the outside of his thigh, beginning to tremble in anticipation. His thighs flexed as his hips moved forward and his grunt mingled with my gasp as he entered me, pushing inside until our hips met. The feeling was uncomfortable at first, but he moved slowly, helping to turn the slight burn into pure bliss. His chest lowered to mine, our bodies completely meshed together. His fluid thrusts remained calm and gentle, erasing every horrible memory I'd experienced sexually with Rod.

Our lips met, locking together, tongues caressing with the slow motion of his hips. The connection was overwhelming, shoving me into his heart, my conscience screaming at me to never let this man go.

With my pulse racing and my muscles clenching, Mitch's movements became quicker along with his breath. He twitched, his ass flexing as he let go inside of me. With a deep breath, he settled on top of me, his chin nuzzling affectionately into my neck. Gentle kisses peppered below my ear, completely relaxing me to satisfaction.

"Tell me you missed me," he murmured into my neck.

I turned my head so I could look at him. His hand found my jaw, massaging my face and brushing the sweaty hair from my forehead. Instead of answering him, I kissed him, rolling so we were on our sides.

"That's not really an answer," he chuckled in between kisses, "but I'll assume it means you did."

I snuggled into his chest as he rolled to his back, wrapping his arm around me so I was tucked into his side. "Tell me something I don't know about you."

My ear found the beat of his heart, a soothing sound that made my heart open, ready to shed some of my ugly. "I had a brother," I whispered, emotion thick in my throat.

Mitch's hand stilled in my hair, then continued stroking the back of my scalp. It was amazing and helped me to relax.

"Besides the three younger ones?"

"He was my Irish twin. We were eleven months apart. He was in the Air Force and he loved it. That's all he'd ever talk about when we were kids. He wanted to fly." A tear rolled down my cheek and onto Mitch's chest.

"So you do know what it's like to lose someone you love," Mitch said gently, still stroking my hair. I nodded, taking a deep breath. "I'm sorry you lost him." My hand curled around his waist, but he reached for it with his free hand, lacing our fingers and kissing each knuckle.

"Do you believe in heaven?" I asked.

He was quiet for a moment. "Yes, I think our loved ones are looking down on us, making sure that when God says it's our time, they're there to greet us with open arms."

Nuzzling him again, I said, "I like to think he's flying, protecting our family and friends. Just like he would if he were still here. Maybe he's even in his uniform. He died in it after all," I sighed, needing to stop talking before I broke down and ruined our post-coital moment.

"I bet he is," Mitch soothed. "I bet he's flying over us right now, his missiles pointing directly at me."

I snorted, a mix of crying and laughter combined. Mitch laughed at my reaction, lovingly kissing my forehead. He began playing with my hand, intertwining and untwining our fingers, pressing the pads together, then tracing circles on my palm. The touch was methodical, and watching was making me sleepy. "Can I stay?" I asked with a yawn.

Mitch's hand still against mine, his arm tightening around my shoulders. "If you get out of this bed before it's light out, I'll tackle you."

"Hmm," I groaned as my eyes began to close.

He was the first man I'd be okay with tackling me for his own pleasure.

CHAPTER SIX

A heavy body covered mine as I laid on my stomach, cozy in the sheets. Warm breath caressed my neck, lips beginning to trace a trail down my spine and back.

"Mmm, that feels nice," I groaned.

Hands replaced the sensual caresses of lips, becoming firmer as they moved from my butt to my shoulders. I was in pure heaven, enjoying the massage. The steady movement of hands changed to a more rapid pace, squeezing harder.

"Ah, getting out the knots, are you?" I winced, wiggling against the mattress.

The course hands found their way past my shoulders to the back of my neck, squeezing harder, causing me discomfort. I squirmed, beginning to feel uneasy as the other hand pressed my stomach further into the mattress. Attempting to move turned difficult, only causing his hands to work my body harder.

"Mitch, that hurts," I mumbled into the pillow.

Suddenly, my head was yanked backward by my hair, causing me to gasp, my hands immediately pushing to my sides. The hard body above me flattened, pinning me down, holding my other hand securely. My insides tightened as fear filled my bones.

"I told you to stay the fuck away from him."

My body flew upright on the bed, reaching for the front of my throat protectively as I gasped for air. I was trembling, a cold sweat forming on the back of my neck. My brown eyes frantically searched the room, trying to comprehend where I was and what had just happened.

I sighed in relief, hugging myself to find comfort. Once my eyes found Mitch, watching his back gently rise with his steady breaths, the pounding of my heart began to slow. He looked so peaceful; a feeling I longed to share with him.

The room was beginning to lighten, the sun was still making its way to start the day. I stood from the bed, walking toward the window. Rod was out there somewhere, but I was prepared to play his game. He'd shed blood once already, and I knew he wouldn't be afraid to do it again, but this time, he wouldn't get away with it. I wouldn't let him hurt the ones I loved.

"I thought I told you not to leave this bed," a groggy voice muffled by the pillows said.

My lip twitched, glancing back toward him. He was facing away from me, head buried in the pillows. "I thought you were going to tackle me if I did?" I said slyly, making my way back into the bed. I curled into his side, causing him to rotate and cuddle me back.

"I'm too tired," he yawned, his arms bulging as they caged me.

I giggled. "Did I wear you out last night?"

One eye opened to examine me. "Maybe the second time."

I kissed his neck, ready to rock his world again. "I haven't tasted all of you yet," I flirted, my hand skimming down the tight bumps of his abdomen.

"Mmm, Jamie Rae, making all of my dreams a reality," he sighed, moving one arm behind his head to get comfortable.

"I was talking about your toes," I teased.

Mitch glanced down at me, taking my wandering hand in his and wrapping it around his thick cock, showing me the motion he liked. "I bet you were."

I came to my knees, working my hand faster after he let go and moved his arm back behind his head. My hand let go abruptly, tracing its way downward as I moved to the end of the bed. "Yes, I need to taste your ankles, your shins, knees, thighs..."

He stuffed a few pillows under his head so he could watch me. "Oh yeah?"

My lips pressed against his big toe, then traveled to his ankle, my eyes never leaving his mischievous grin. The moment I stuck my tongue out to lick up his shins and circle his knee, his chest puffed, his grin fading into lust.

"You sure know how to work that mouth."

I smiled, kissing my way up his thighs. Once I reached his pride and joy, I studied it, my chest rising and falling at a faster pace. I wanted to taste him, excited about the way his eyes would roll to the back of his head and how his body would shiver. "Is there something you want?" I asked seductively, mimicking his words from earlier.

He sat up on his elbows, looking at me intently. "Put it in your mouth, Jamie."

"It?" I asked innocently, my salacious grin in place.

He moved one hand to the back of my neck, eyes boring into mine. "I want the tip of my cock to feel the back of your throat." His voice was deep and commanding, telling me I should do as I was told. I licked my lips in anticipation as my hands moved up his muscular thighs. The urge for this moment to lock in his brain for the rest of his life was a goal I needed to obtain. I wanted to make him crave this feeling for the rest of his life.

One hand grasped him firmly, my tongue traced my teeth as a tease. His chest rumbled while his hand tensed around the back of my neck. My eyes were still entranced with his, enjoying the way his jaw ticked in anticipation. I jerked my hand faster, making his blood pump fully.

"Jamie, stop fucking teas—"

Mitch hissed as my mouth came crashing down on him, taking no precautions or reservations. Groaning loudly, his hand moved from my neck to my hair, pulling it from my face so he could watch me devour him. Both my hand and mouth were working in unison, my mouth sucking rapidly as my tongue flicked and swirled. I covered my teeth with my lips, taking him farther than I'd taken any man willingly.

"That's it, take all of it," he commanded, his voice feral and full of need.

I loved every moment of it until his hand pulled at my hair, his hips beginning to move upward as I took him in my mouth. Flashbacks of Rod forcing me to go down on him invaded my memory. My attempt to push them away was impossible, remembering wanting to stop, but he'd hold my head, forcing me to go deeper.

A gag escaped me as I thought about Rod, my body tensing remembering his torment.

Mitch's hips stopped, his hand letting go of my hair. I pulled back, my trembling lips kissing his hip as a distraction from my brain. I didn't want to stop making Mitch feel good, but my head was playing games with me.

"Whoa, sorry, you okay?" he breathed, stroking my cheek.

I nodded, my hands pushing his body so he was lying on his back. I had to regain control to get out of this state of mind.

Mitch fought me, rolling so he was pinning me on my stomach. "That was fucking amazing, now it's my turn," he promised against my ear. His lips trailed down my back, reminding me of the dream I'd had only moments ago. Sweat formed on my skin as he reached my behind, gently nipping each cheek as he positioned himself behind me. My hands reached for the pillow, rubbing the soft threads for comfort. *He wasn't going to hurt me*, my brain reassured, but I pictured Rod laughing behind my conscience.

Rough hands grasped my hips, pulling them upward so I was on my knees. My legs trembled, fearful what was going to happen next. His cock laid heavy on my ass while his front pressed against my back, giving kisses that were meant to feel sweet and affection to the back of my neck.

"You've got a nice ass," he murmured against my ear. I gulped as my nerves took over. "Relax, baby," he said sweetly, the tension in my body obvious.

The tone of his voice should have eased me, but my heart wouldn't stop racing. All I could picture was Rod forcing himself behind me, slurring demeaning words and threats as he'd pump forcefully inside of me. Mitch reached for my jaw, gently caressing with his hand as his lips found my neck. His hips began searching and my body instinctively moved forward, fighting him. Suddenly, his hands were too close, his body was surrounding me, and I couldn't get out. I clawed the pillow, wanting to escape the dark and scary place my mind had drifted too.

Mitch's hand released from my jaw. "Jamie?"

When I didn't answer, he moved to my side, his hand moving over the length of my back. My knees fell to the bed, curling underneath my stomach as I hugged the pillow.

"Jamie, what's wrong?" Mitch asked, his hands reaching to pull me closer to him.

Tears ran down my cheeks into the pillow. My head was playing a video of Rod ramming me from behind, laughing as his hands pinned down my shoulders. *It wouldn't go away.*

"Jamie!" Mitch shouted, yanking me from the pillow and onto his lap.

My eyes sprung open, Rod's demonic laugh morphed into Mitch's panic-stricken face. "I'm sorry," I choked, mad at myself for letting the monster control my thoughts.

Mitch's hands cradled my face. "Sorry for what? Did I hurt you? Could you not breathe?" My arms latched around his shoulders for comfort as I came back to the now. I couldn't let Mitch see my past; he'd run far away from the stupid teenage girl who'd let a man control her and ruin her life. His arms hooked around me, rocking me back and forth to help calm me. I was thankful for his silence the next few minutes while I collected my thoughts. "I'm sorry, I just wasn't sure what you were going to do," I finally mumbled into his shoulder.

"Tell me to stop next time," he said softly, his hand cupping the back of my head as it rested on his shoulder. "The way your body was shaking, I thought you were excited until I saw you were crying. The last thing I ever want to do is make you feel uncomfortable."

I nodded into his neck, squeezing him tighter. Calloused hands found my cheeks, pulling me from the crook where I'd found comfort. Forcing me to meet his gaze, he said, "I could be three thrusts away from coming, and I'd stop if you asked. Do you understand?"

The sincerity in his words helped to warm my body from the distress it had just gone through. "Yes, I believe you."

He gave me a genuine smile. "How about I go make breakfast? You can stay in bed if you'd like and I'll bring it to you."

I returned his smile, climbing under the covers. He stood from the bed, retrieving his boxers and sliding them on. I'd be lying if I said it wasn't fun to watch. With a gentleness I wasn't used to, he tucked me in the covers, kissing me softly. "I hope you like French toast."

Mitch stopped by the nightstand, grabbing my phone. "Looks like Daddy's texting you," he said with a smirk while tossing me the phone before he left for the kitchen.

I furrowed my brows, curious why my dad would text me, and if he actually knew how to text. I shook my head when I saw it was Nathan.

Nathan: **You going to make it to the meeting at 10? If not we'll manage.**

I probably could.

Nathan: **If you're currently lying in my brother's bed, I'm not expecting to see you the rest of the day.**

How the hell did he know? Oh well, I wanted to give Mitch a chance. There was no shame in hiding it.

Maybe the rest of the week...

Nathan: **Now let's not get carried away.**

I chuckled.

I know, I'll see you on the plane Tuesday morning.

Nathan: **Figured. I don't want to hear about how shitty of a lay my brother is ;0)**

Fighting the tingling between my legs was hard. Thinking about how amazing his head was between my legs would stick with me for a while.

There's no need to tell you how good of a carpet muncher your brother is.

Nathan: **GROSS. See you tomorrow.**

CHAPTER SEVEN

Mitch and I stayed in the rest of the day and night. He'd blown off visiting a construction site in Ludington to stay with me. Usually, I wouldn't encourage such behavior, but I was being greedy now and wanted to get lost in him.

He'd cooked three meals, and had impressed me with each one.

His gentleness was heartwarming, especially when he was one who liked control as much as I did. The night had gone by too quickly, and I needed to head to the airport in a few hours. Mitch was already moving around, freshly showered and making coffee.

"Here you are, cream and sugar, masking the taste of coffee. I'll have to get some of that flavored shit for you," he teased, handing me a mug.

I grinned, then took a sip. "I don't know how you drink it black."

"It's to wake me up, not give me a sugar rush."

I giggled. His smile was sincere as he reached for my cheek. "What are we? I don't want to play games, Jamie. I want this, more than just when you lose the feeling to fight wanting to be with me."

"I don't fight you." My voice was small. He'd nailed it on the head, but I was done fighting my feelings for him.

"I love you, Jamie."

My eyes were wide and I was at a loss for words. I'd only said those words to one other man besides my father, and he'd had a fucked up version of what love was.

"I know I just took a huge chance by telling you that, but it's the truth. Ever since you started working in Miami, I've been enamored with you. At first, I did just want you physically. But then I got to know you and your witty, no bullshit attitude. It was sexy as hell. I love to argue with you, but I love your soft side when you let me hold and protect you. You hold your own, yet you're willing to be held by me as well."

Both of Mitch's hands found their way to my cheeks, his thumbs stroking each side. "You don't have to say anything, but I needed you to know before you got on that plane with Nathan to go back to Miami. I'll be there in a few days, okay? Maybe we can have dinner?"

"I'd like that," I choked, not wanting him to leave. My brain couldn't wrap around my words fast enough to tell him how I felt. He leaned in to kiss me, opening his mouth for me to come and explore. My hands wrapped around his shoulders, holding him as tight as I could. Reluctantly, I pulled away.

"Going back to Miami won't change my mind about giving us a shot."

He offered me a small smile, and I knew he was guarding his heart, afraid I'd change my mind. I'd screwed him over before, so I didn't blame him for being apprehensive.

"Text me when you land."

I nodded, kissing him one last time before he left.

***

Nathan ended up taking a separate flight back to Miami. It was probably better since I'd been woozy the entire flight. When I arrived at my condo, I expected to find one of those stupid ass letters, but nothing was on the doorstep. I'd even expected something to be inside my condo since Rod seemed to be a ghost and could get anywhere he wanted.

But there was nothing.

I couldn't contain the smug smile that crossed my face. Maybe he'd realized that I wasn't afraid of him anymore and was ready to fight back for my life, just as my older brother had ordered with his last breath.

Nathan: **Taking a red eye in tomorrow night. Can we do breakfast the following morning?**

I smiled. I was sure he was treating the breakfast as a meeting, but would most likely give me shit about Mitch. He was typically all business, but when it came to his family, he felt privileged enough to be involved.

Sure. Guess I can hold down the office without you until then.

Nathan: **Don't miss me too much. Text you with a time later.**

Mitch would be in town that day, and I couldn't wait to see him. I'd missed him the moment he left, walking out the door in his work boots, worn jeans, and white shirt. He was so sexy, even with shorter hair that I had to really grasp to tug on. My heart fluttered. Was this what love was supposed to be like? Then my stomach dropped again.

Maybe it was just the stomach flu.

***

I felt nauseated the following day, but I blamed it on a questionable bagel from the airport. After lounging around my condo, I decided to call Mitch. I'd wanted to call him the second I was free but didn't want to come across as a needy girlfriend—if that was what I was. *Girlfriend...* I'd had my fair share of partners, but never considered myself a girlfriend because of Rod. The feeling made me feel girly.

"Hey, beautiful," Mitch greeted.

I rolled my eyes. "How do you know I look beautiful?"

"You could be hungover and hit in the face with a baseball bat and you'd still be beautiful."

I chuckled. "And if I had the stomach flu?"

"Hmm, that's a tough call..."

"I've been puking on and off the past few days. I think I ate something bad," I sighed.

"I'm sorry. Why didn't you tell me earlier? I'd have taken an earlier flight in. Tony can handle my work here."

I smiled, feeling warm and fuzzy for his need to take care of me.

"As sexy as it sounds seeing you catch my puke, I think I'll survive on my own. I'm feeling better now."

"Good, I'll be in tomorrow morning. Come pick me up?"

"Of course."

"I'm excited to see you," he said quietly.

More flutters filled my stomach. "I'm excited to see you too."

***

My mind was foggy all night, but not from confusion. I'd come to an epiphany last night, and for more than one major life event. I needed to see Becca, but she was busy, so I'd tell Nathan first.

The flutters weren't the stomach flu. It was Mitch, all of him. He was consuming my mind in the most complete way. We were each others equal halves. We were both hard-headed but had worked our way toward knowing when to give to each other. He was everything physically I'd dreamed of, and his heart and mind only rounded him more. His intellect was hidden from the world, but I managed to find it through all the bullshit.

He knew me inside and out as well, called me on my crap when I was being irrational. He knew when to be firm and when to be soft with me, and didn't push my demons to the surface. He was waiting for me to confront them and was patient enough to hold my hand until that time would come.

I was in love with Mitch Conklin.

Nathan was sitting at the corner table in the coffee shop in his typical pristine Prada suit, coffee in front of him and a newspaper in the other hand. "It's been a while," I said, crossing my arms. My red shift dress felt powerful as I stood in front of him. I'd put it on for Mitch; he loved me in red.

He glanced up from his newspaper, smiled, then continued his attention on the black and white lettering. "That's what happens when one gets wrapped up in the sheets with a Conklin."

***

"You're sure?" Nathan asked as though I was crazy. I nodded like an idiot, happier than I'd ever felt. He shook his head in defeat. "All right, it's your life, live it how you want."

Even though his words were stern, he gave me a knowing grin. Nathan would forever be supportive of me and all of my decisions. He knew his little brother too and wanted the best for him as well.

His phone beeped.

"Odd. Kobiashi wants us to meet him at his new building of condos. Has a question about the suite."

My eyes furrowed. I knew Mitch had been busy, but Kobiashi also knew the suite was going to be delayed because of the rather large adjustments to the drafts he demanded. "Did he say something was wrong?"

"No, it's from his assistant. They want to meet in an hour." Nathan looked down at his watch. "We should get going."

I stood from my seat. "Yeah, I need to go get Mitch from the airport soon."

Nathan stood with me, pulling out his wallet to pay for breakfast. "He's going to need to take a cab. Kobiashi wants both of us there."

"Why me?"

Nathan shrugged. "Maybe he's on the Jamie Rae fantasy train." Nathan raised a brow at me waiting for a smart ass comment to come from my mouth.

"We both know only two men have fantasies about me," I flirted. Nathan gave me a confused look. "You, and your sexy as hell brother." I laughed, hitting him in the bicep.

He wrapped an arm around my shoulders. "I don't munch on carpets. Therefore, my interest in you is purely business."

I laughed and wrapped my arm around his waist as we left the restaurant. "Let me text Mitch." I knew he'd be disappointed. So would I. I couldn't wait to have his big, strong arms wrap around me.

I have to meet with Nathan and Kobiashi at Plaza Towers. I won't be able to pick you up from the airport. :0(Call you when I'm done. I can't wait to see you.

I wanted to add I love you at the end, but I'd rather whisper it in his ear after I'd ridden him. My insides tightened at the thought.

The skies were almost pure black, a storm threatening as we drove. You could see lightening off in the distance, and hear the quiet rumble that followed.

"It's funny, I thought more people would be here," Nathan said as we pulled into the parking lot of the Plaza Towers. No one was moving around which was odd for a Conklin Construction site on a Wednesday morning.

"Where the hell is everyone?" Nathan sounded pissed.

"Maybe they're taking an early lunch, or called it a day because it's about to storm."

"The building's enclosed, no reason a storm would stop them. We live in Florida for Christ's sake." He shook his head. "We're early, but I want to check and see how far along the building is." He jumped out of the car and walked quickly through the main entrance. "The fucking door is unlocked! These little punks are going to get an earful when they get back."

I rolled my eyes at him. Most likely the workers were up in the suite, busily working on Kobiashi's demands, and I was in too good of a mood to get irritated by something so small.

We made our way to the elevator, Nathan mumbling the entire time about responsibility and professionalism. The elevator doors opened, revealing the half-finished space. More was done than the last time I'd seen it, but I also know it had to be completely taken apart. The framework was hard to work around since it was such a tall building. Mitch had to think smartly to get all of Kobiashi's demands correct, and I was proud of him for managing the situation so well.

As we walked through the threshold of the building, the lights flickered, along with a massive boom of thunder. A zipping sound occurred, then the lights went out completely.

"You've got to be fucking kidding me," Nathan shouted. The storm was swallowing the light now, and we couldn't see a thing. He pulled out his phone, searching for the flashlight app.

"Do you know where the breaker is?" I asked, pulling out my phone.

"I've got no fucking idea." He was grumpy now, and the urge to giggle was a hard one to stop. Angry people looked so silly when you felt like you were on top of the world.

"I'll check this way while you go that way," Nathan grumbled, going in the opposite direction.

I searched the huge space, daydreaming about getting my own place, one where Mitch would be a permanent fixture. "I don't see it over this way," I yelled, but only the sound of my heels clicked loudly. An eerie feeling swept through me, surrounding me in this large space.

"Nathan?"

I searched each room, shadows startling me along the way. Then my eye caught a leg, and I rushed into the room. Nathan was on the ground, holding his side as blood gushed over his hands.

"Nathan! Oh my God!" I rushed to his side, nearly stumbling over pieces of plywood and metal rods.

"It's not... that... bad..." Nathan choked, attempting to sit up, but fell backward in pain. He let out a loud groan of agony. Tears swelled my eyes as they followed the puddle of blood that was forming. "You need... to go..." he muttered, wincing in pain.

"No! What happened?" I shouted, searching for something to help stop the bleeding from his side. I went to find a rag in the other room, calling 911 in the process. Of course, the phone was taking forever to connect as I zoomed back to Nathan.

"Jamie, you have to....leave," he pressed. I ignored him, holding pressure to his wound, causing him to let out another sound of agony. His scream was muffled by a roar of thunder.

"Someone did this..." he choked, beginning to cough.

That familiar chill ran up my spine. My breath hitched, afraid to turn around. It was Rod. This was how he was punishing me for going against his will, by hurting the ones I loved, again. Tears sprung from my eyes as the 911 operator answered. I refused to lose Nathan as I'd lost Landon. "I'm not leaving you," I said, staring into Nathan's blue eyes. But the blue was fading; he needed the bleeding to stop or else I was going to lose him. "Don't you dare give up."

"Ma'am, how can I help you?" the 911 operated asked sternly.

"Yes, I need an ambulance at the Tower Plaza. I have a thirty-two year old male with a bad wound. It's bleeding, a lot," I choked, trying to stay strong.

"I'll send someone right away. What happened to him?" she asked calmly, the sound of rapid typing in the background.

"I'm not sure." I fought back tears, watching the blood soak through the rag. "It won't stop bleeding!"

Nathan's eyelids were heavy. The phone fell from my ear as I took Nathan's face in my hands. "Don't you dare close your eyes," I threatened, gently shaking his face, his blue eyes staring up at me. His face was cold, along with his hand that moved to touch my forearm.

"Jamie... Go... I'll be..." He coughed again, and a trickle of blood fell from his nose.

No, no, no, no, no, no!

Images of Landon's head laying lifeless in my lap slapped me in my face. How the light drained from his eyes as Nathan's blue eyes were fading now. "Nathan, please," I begged, holding his head in my lap as I'd held Landon's, my own flesh and blood.

Nathan coughed again, but this time blood landed on my dress, matching the deadly red color.

Anger filled me. Fuck, Rod! He was taking another man from my life that I loved. He wasn't going to get away with it this time.

I leaned down to Nathan's cold lips. "You're going to be fine." The ambulance would be here soon, and I needed to take care of my past. "I love you," I whispered, fighting the thick emotion that was feuding with my rage.

"Jay… no…" he rasped again, his eyes finally closing. I held his head close to my lap, kissing his cheeks and lips, sorry for ever getting close to anyone, dragging them into my tortured life to be slain like a helpless pig at the butchering farm.

"I'm so sorry," I whispered past my tears.

With one last goodbye kiss to my best friend, I laid him down in his own puddle of blood, thunder blasting in the background with the loud thumping of rain on the windows.

I was done hiding from this asshole. He needed to be gone from my life and the rest of the world so he couldn't hurt anyone again. I picked up a metal rod from the floor that I'd tripped on earlier, prepared to take the life from the asshole who stole mine.

Lightning flashed through the condo, masking the shadows that lurked. "I'm right here you asshole, come and get me," I growled, gripping the rod tightly in both hands.

Then the voice that caused so much terror appeared through the darkness. "Oh, Jamie Rae, I thought I told you red wasn't your color."

Thud.

My head took a heavy blow out of nowhere, blurring my vision in the darkness. Dizziness set in as my body crashed to the ground, forcefully slamming the life out of me. I saw stars, just as I'd seen them lying in the safety of Mitch's arms on top of his condo, lost in the sky with the Greek gods.

CHAPTER EIGHT

Rod

She was light in my arms, her head lolled over my bicep as I carried her with quick strides to the elevator. The metal rod I'd hit her with caused a knot to rise on the side of her head instantly. I crinkled my brows as I stared down at her beautiful face and the wave of her soft caramel hair, trying to reign in my anger.

The way she looked at him, cried for him, let his blood cover her...

It was too much.

She loved that man, but I was the only one allowed to have her heart.

Shoving the knife in his side, twisting it deeper while watching his eyes widen with fear was exhilarating, the best revenge I could get. The last kick to his temple to shut him up after I hit Jamie over the head had sealed the deal. He might have made it if he could have kept his mouth shut, but I doubted it. Watching the blood drain from his lifeless body after pounding him with my fist in the face felt too amazing.

That face kissed my woman. Probably in too many places. He had to die.

Count to ten.

Blowing air out, I'm brought back to the now, running through all the small details in my head. Jamie's knocked out cold, but I couldn't rely on that. She needed to be unconscious until we got home.

To our home.

I smiled as I gazed at her features, guilt filling me for not going with the original plan. The syringe was in my pocket, but as usual, my emotions had gotten the best of me.

Nathan Conklin.

He was always too close to her. Opening her door, setting his hand on the small of her back, staying at her place. I almost pulled out my 22 Glock from my holster hidden under my hoodie and shot the pretty boy right then and there.

When I first caught sight of her spending time with him, I thought they were merely work associates, but soon his car had been parked at the ramp of her condo too often.

Then one night the two of them were coming home from a night out, wrapped in each others arms. The dreamy look in her eyes as she pouted her lips, begging for him to kiss her, the red point of her heel rising as his arm snaked behind her back.

Red. I fucking hate that color.

My mother always wore red, and the deep hue made me grind my teeth.

Jamie knew I hated that color, but she never followed my rules.

Just like my mother.

And grandmother.

And grandfather.

But they weren't an issue anymore.

Now I had Jamie. She was going to be mine for as long as we both lived, a promise I was planning to keep.

The rain poured down as I shoved the back fire exit door open with my shoulder, quickly finding my car. Using the window to help prop Jamie up, I opened the rear driver side door, then slid her inside as carefully as I could.

"We're going to be so happy," I whispered, running my hand through her hair and gently brushing the large egg on her head as I stroked her tender locks.

Slamming the door shut and clicking the lock button, I took one final glance around the back alley behind the Plaza Towers. No way my plan could be compromised, not at this point. I had too many situations, too many theories and reasons for my life to finally fall into place.

For our *life* to fall into place.

Water dripped from my hood as I moved to the outskirts of the alley, stepping one heavy boot one after the other. There was a piece of my plan, standing underneath an awning and rubbing her shoulders for warmth. A frown crossed my face as I walked faster to approach her.

"Why isn't your hair down?" I hissed.

Her eye-roll peeved me, but I let it slide. I didn't have much time. Pulling a car key from my pocket, I asked, "Did you get everything I sent?"

She nodded as she let the caramel tendrils of hair out of her ponytail. Worry filled her scowl. "When will I see you again?"

"I'm not sure. Did you understand the instructions?"

Her scowl deepened. "I'm not incompetent."

She had that attitude that made me wild, just like my love in the back seat of my car. "I know. Now go."

"But when will I see--"

"Shh. A man will meet you at the border. I'll contact you as soon as I can." She reached for me, but I grabbed her wrists before she could wrap them around my waist. "Go. There isn't much time." Her lip quivered slightly from the unknown, but softened once I stroked her cheek.

Her eyes longed for me as they gazed at my lips, but I took a step back, giving us some distance. Kissing her goodbye wasn't part of the plan. She'd already touched me too many times. This body was Jamie's now, not hers.

"Now go," I commanded while stepping away. Her head dipped low as she crossed the street in the pouring rain to Jamie's car, pointing the keys to unlock it. Once she was safely in the car and off in the right direction, I ran back down the alley to Jamie.

The car door creaked as I slid inside, followed by a loud boom of thunder. I checked my rearview mirror to see Jamie was still out. I'd have to sedate her when we got home. She didn't need to be in pain from my fucked up judgment with the metal rod any longer than she had to be. Besides, I'd need a few more hours for everything to fall into place.

The tires squealed as I spun out of sight, leaving no traces of our whereabouts. I was an invisible man, and now Jamie was going to be my invisible woman.

CHAPTER NINE

Mitch

I'd never fallen so hard for a woman in my life.

She'd chewed me up and spit me back out more than once, but her resistance only pulled me in, and now she was willing to give us a try. I was a magnet to her, prepared to drop everything in my world just to have a fraction of her time.

I tried to call Jamie and Nathan, but Jamie's cell was only a dial tone while Nathan's rang but went to voicemail. Nathan always answered his phone. *Always.*

Something wasn't right.

There was no reason for Jamie and Nathan to go to the Plaza Towers and meet Kobiashi.. For the most part, it was finished and ready for the designers to come in and do their thing. I checked my calendar, and sure enough, the site would be empty today

The ping of the seatbelt sign went off, and I bolted, nearly knocking over the older woman across from me while grabbing my carry-on bag. I gave her an apologetic wave, then wedged my way to the front of the plane and into the terminal.

"Pick up your phone," I muttered under my breath after I called Nathan for the tenth time since the plane had landed. I made it to the pick-up lane, waving down the closest taxi.

My mind was reeling as I watched the rain fall on the window. Was Kobiashi pulling a fast one on us? Complaining about my work to Nathan, *the boss man*. I bit the insides of my cheeks. Kobiashi was a power hungry asshole, always trying to get under my skin. I wasn't willing to just tell him yes whenever he wanted. *Maybe he sees me as a threat?*

You still with Kobiashi? I texted Nathan.

No response. *How far up Kobiashi's ass is he?*

The Tower Plaza was deserted as it should be. Only Nathan's car was parked on the street. They probably rode together. My grin couldn't be contained. Just seeing her would satisfy the ache. Touching her would help too, but she was professional and wouldn't go for PDA in front of a client or my brother.

All those good feelings I had about Jamie began to melt as I stepped foot into the main lobby. The air was cool and the generator lights were on, meaning the power went out from the storm. My pace quickened toward the elevator, thankful the backup generator had enough energy to power it. To my luck, the door opened, but my heart sank.

The elevator should not have been on the main floor. It should have been up at the penthouse, descending when I pushed the button. Something deep in my gut told me I needed to get to that penthouse as fast as possible.

My breathing sped up with each passing floor, paranoid the little bit of power we had left was going to shut off and trap me in this confined space. After what felt like an eternity, the elevator doors slid open to the darkened lobby. Taking one more deep breath, I walked through the doors and across the threshold to the penthouse, making a mental note to figure out why the doors hadn't been installed. I knew they were custom built, but they'd arrived nearly a week ago. *Just proves if you want something done right you've got to do it yourself.*

I clenched my jaw as I searched the dimly lit space...

And found Nathan, in a bloody heap on the floor.

"Nathan!" I fell to my knees at his side, searching him with my hands to find out what had happened. His face was

distorted as though he'd taken multiple blows from heavy objects, open wounds making him barely recognizable.

My stomach twisted as a puddle of dark liquid reached my jeans, soaking me with my brother's blood. "Nathan! Can you hear me? *Nathan!*"

His eyes slightly opened, then rolled to the back of his head.

Finding the blood trail, I pressed down on the large gash in his side. He was alive, but barely. "You're going to be okay," I stuttered. Of all the times I needed to be strong, this was the most important.

The sound of a dial tone broke through the fast beat of the blood pumping to my heart. The icy shiver traveled down my spine as I turned to see where the sound was coming from.

Jamie.

"Where's Jamie? Is she here?" My voice cracked as I swung my head to search past the gentle glow of her phone, but it was pointless. It was still too dark to see.

Nathan tried to talk, but blood trickled from his lips.

"Shh, it's okay. I'll figure it out," I whispered, leaning closer to my older brother. "Don't talk, hold on to your strength."

He made a gagging noise, his body beginning to tremble and fidget. He wanted to communicate with me, but he was fading. *Fast.*

Keeping one hand on Nathan's wound, I reached into my back pocket, pulling my phone to call an ambulance. "I'll be right back."

"Jamie!" I called out, sprinting through the penthouse. I searched each room, making it to the other side by the time the 911 operator answered.

"911 what's your emergency?"

"I need an ambulance at Plaza Towers, the penthouse suite. My brother, he's been attacked." My breath was ragged as I sped through each room. "He's bleeding from his side."

Fuck. Where was she?

After looking briefly through the rooms, I'd found my way to Nathan. "He's beat up really bad," I croaked, kneeling back down beside him.

"It appears we have an ambulance on route to that destination. Is your brother conscious?" the operator asked.

Just as she said it, his slightly opened lids fell closed.

A flash of lightning appeared, followed by the boom of thunder. The feeling of tiny needles poking every inch of my skin arose, the pressure building as I observed my oldest brother. I held my breath, not prepared for what my eyes would see.

His chest that had been heaving, fighting for air, slowed to a complete stop.

My hand froze on the gash in his side as I watched the small bit of life drain from his body. "I think he just stopped breathing," I gasped, bending down further so I could listen. His body was cold as ice, his lips turning blue as they stilled.

"Sir?"

No sound, no movement. His body lay there, stiff as a board, bleeding and broken. He'd been pulled from this world, but I was willing to fight the hand that was trying to take him from me.

Now I was in a whirlwind, my mind going into hyper drive in reaction to this messed up situation. Throwing my phone, I ripped the buttons off his dress shirt, then forced his limp and lifeless body flat on his back.

"I'm not losing you, too," I said confidently as memories of my father lying in the coffin blurred my vision. He was the rock that held me together when my father passed, giving me tough love yet supporting me the best he could.

My hands pressed against his chest. "Come on, Nathan!" I shouted, the palms of my hands pressing harder, trying to pulse his heart back to life. My biceps flexed with each press to his heart, begging for a response.

Crack.

His body flinched and for a second I stopped, an ounce of hope that I'd done right by my brother, giving him that breath of life again.

Leaning down, there was no movement, no soft breaths of air releasing from his nose or lips.

"Fuck!" My palms found his chest again. "I can't lose you, Nathan."

I pushed and pushed, imagining the blood flowing to his heart, pleading for it to beat again.

God, please... I need him.

Crack.

I'd paused from the sound again, but still no sign of life from his unconscious state. My silent prayers felt ignored, the sense of loss and pain already consuming my body. The angel of death was near, his presence surrounding me with gloom. I'd lost my father, now my brother was on the edge of my fingertips, on the verge of falling into another world.

Then I saw the white light, Nathan's saving grace into heaven. I blinked hard, my hands never losing rhythm on Nathan's chest. The light wasn't a tunnel to heaven. It was a flashlight.

"Emergency medical technician. If you can hear me, make noise."

"Over here!" I shouted, a small bit of hope surfacing into my heart. "He's stopped breathing."

The medics rushed to either side of me, one fluidly searching through his bag.

One pressed his fingers to Nathan's neck. "Let me," he commanded once he couldn't find a pulse, firmly nudging me away with his shoulder, his latex-covered hands taking the place of mine. "Get the AED."

The muscles in my arms tightened as my hands found the back of my neck. I felt useless.

"Let's give him a jump," the medic stated, beginning to stick wires on Nathan's chest and side while the other kept pumping his chest. It was a defibrillator, the last ditch effort for survival.

"Stand clear," the medic said in unison with the defibrillator.

My hands stayed on the back of my neck, my chest coming to a halt.

Why the hell was it taking so long? Was this thing broken?

Analyzing heart rhythm.

He had a rhythm. There was hope. They could save him.

Shock advised.

More moments passed, then a long beep followed by Nathan's body jolting off the ground. I jumped backward, startled by the lunge of his body.

Repeat CPR.

"Still no pulse."

The medic who had attached the defibrillator began chest compressions as instructed.

Crack.

The EMT ignored the sound and kept pumping Nathan's chest. "It's his ribs. Rather have broken ribs than a beatless heart."

I gulped, nodding in agreement, not questioning if I'd pushed him too hard earlier.

Shock advised.

"Don't touch him," the medic reminded, throwing his hand out in front of me. My body was frozen, waiting to take a breath as soon as Nathan could.

Another blast from the AED created tremors through Nathan's body.

Analyzing...

My body quaked as I watched the EMTs glance at each other. If the third shock didn't work, the outcome wouldn't be good.

Most likely he'd be six feet under in a plot next to our dad.

How was I going to tell Tyler? How was I going to tell Mom?

Mom. She'd be devastated.

Shock advised.

"Oh my God," I choked, my hands finding my face as I began to panic. My heart pounded louder, the blood burning through my ears as I rocked back and forth. I couldn't do this. I wasn't the strong one. The strong one was lying in his own puddle of blood.

The sound of his body leaving the floor and smacking back down caused my skin to tremble more. *Please, God. Save him.*

Repeat CPR.

"Come on, buddy," the EMT said sternly, his hands driving back into Nathan's chest. "Now's the time to fight."

Nathan was a fighter, the toughest man I'd known.

"Nathan," I whispered one last time, licking the tears that dripped down my cheeks like acid, burning my tongue.

Analyzing...

The medics exchanged glances again, and I knew they'd lost hope. The third time was the charm, not the fourth or fifth.

They were probably trying to telepathically choose who'd be the one to pull the plug.

Nothing in life could prepare me for this. Watching my brother die in front of me, not able to do anything but hand him over to our maker.

I wasn't ready…

He couldn't go…

Shock advised.

CHAPTER TEN

Jamie

Warmth surrounded me, a silky sheet with a feather down comforter resting on my sensitive skin. I snuggled a pillow, my hands gripping the sheets tighter as I began to stir. A fogginess clouded my brain, unsure exactly where I was, or if I could even open my eyes. I was so comfortable and relaxed, my body feeling like jello. Except for my head. A dull ache pricked at my scalp, but my arms were too fatigued to move.

A firm yet gentle hand massaged the painful spot on my head, causing me to melt even more into the cozy sheets. "Sleep… a little longer," a deep, husky voice commanded.

That voice…

Fighting the urge to keep my eyes closed and my body still, my heavy lids fluttered open, only to see a man's thigh sitting on the bed next to me.

"Where am I?" My voice faded as I licked my lips, my eyes falling shut again.

"You're home."

Home?

Attempting to sit up and force my eyes to open again was a challenge, but needed to be done. Any weakness in my body turned to fear the second I locked eyes with the man who'd been massaging my head.

My body lunged away from him, attempting to swat his hand away, but I'd missed. My motor skills were off, and I couldn't move away from him fast enough.

Rod shot to his feet, holding both hands in the air. "Stop. You'll make yourself sick. The sedative isn't worn off yet."

"What the hell is going on?" I shouted, searching the room and covering my body. I was only wearing a plain white T-shirt and panties.

Icy blue eyes pinned me to the headboard of the bed, causing me to stop all movement and close my own eyes. This was a dream. It had to be.

"We'll talk once you've slept more."

Slept more? How could I sleep when that monster was near?

I willed my eyes to open again. "What did you do?" My temper was about to rise, fighting whatever drug Rod had given me. I needed to jog my memory and figure out what the fuck had happened.

"Lay down," he commanded, his voice getting deeper.

My hands vigorously rubbed my face. *Wake up!*

A heavy, irritable sigh blew out his nose as he walked toward me. Leaning down, he placed both hands on my biceps, holding them firmly.

I froze.

That touch. At one point, it healed me, sending shivers of excitement. But now, it burned me to the bed, fear creeping slowly through my blood as his thumbs caressed my tense muscles.

I studied his face through heavy lids. He'd matured in the almost seven years I'd been hiding from him. He was bigger, broader. His hair was cut shorter, only a few wet, blond strands pushed to the side of his forehead. His features were sharper, no stubble to his jaw. *But those eyes...* They hadn't changed. That icy blue gaze penetrated into your mind as though they were trying to control you.

"Please," he whispered. "Don't make me do this the hard way."

Hard way? I gulped, my eyes becoming wet as my lip trembled. With as much force as I could muster, I attempted to shrug my shoulders so he'd stop touching me. I needed to get out of here, drugged or not. The room spun as I fought him, my shaky hands pressing against his chest to back away.

"Jamie," he warned as he fought me off. He stood from the bed in unison with my clumsy attempts to escape. I nearly fell, but he caught me with one arm.

"Let go of me. You can't keep me here," I meant to shout, but my voice came out quivering. My fists were curled, trying to find a steady rhythm into his chest so he'd back away and let me leave.

"Hard way it's going to be then."

The firm grasp of his hands on my hips shoved me down on the bed, my arms still flailing towards his direction. He was too strong, especially when I wasn't stable and my vision was blurry. He straddled me, one arm pressed against my chest.

No, not this... please.

Both my hands flew to his wrist, terrified his hand would creep their way to my neck, strangling me until I'd succumbed to his ways. But his hand stayed on my chest while the other reached into his back pocket, pulling a syringe and shoving it into my neck before I could blink.

The grip I had on his forearm loosened as my eyes rolled to the back of my head. My insides were screaming to fight with everything I had, but my body turned to mush, the tidal wave inside of me calming to still waters.

CHAPTER ELEVEN

Mitch

"What's going on?" Tyler's voice was clipped.

My brows pinched hearing the tone of his voice. He was always so grumpy. I still didn't understand how his wife put up with him. I even called him from Nathan's phone, knowing he would have let my phone go to voicemail if he were busy.

It took me a moment to collect my thoughts again. I'd been sitting in the waiting room for a few hours, finally finding the courage to call my older brother. "Hey, it's Mitch. Nathan's...," I gulped. "He's in the hospital."

All I heard was silence on the other end of the line. "Tyler?"

He cleared his throat. "What happened? Is he okay?"

I fought the tremor that coursed through my body. "I don't know."

"I'll be on the next flight to Miami. Let me call Becca, then I'll call you back, all right?" His voice was softer, giving me a small amount of comfort.

"Tyler?"

"Yeah?"

"I don't know if I can call Mom."

He sighed. "Is it that bad?" My silence must have answered his question. "Let me get there, then we'll figure out Mom, okay?"

I nodded as though he could see me.

"I'll call you when I find a flight. Mitch?"

"Yes?" I croaked.

"It'll be okay."

I hung up the phone, hoping to God he was right. My hands found the back of my neck as I put my head between my legs. My mind was racing, spinning in circles, trying to process everything that had happened. The shivers that ran up and down my spine weren't good ones, and a gentle hand could help soothe them. I needed Jamie. But I had no idea where she was. Fear tingled up my spine. What if the fucker who did this to Nathan took her?

A pair of bootie-covered feet approached me, causing me to lift my head and pause my scattered thoughts. "Are you the family of Nathan Conklin?"

I flew to my feet. "Yes. Is he okay?"

"He's stable, for now. The laceration to his lower left abdomen caused severe trauma and he'll be in surgery for the next several hours."

"Several hours?" My voice broke. "But he's going to be okay?"

His dark eyes revealed nothing. "The next twenty-four hours are going to be critical. Once he's out of initial surgery, I'll be able to tell you more. We don't know exactly what damage has been done."

My throat was beyond dry, and swallowing was hard. "What do I do?"

"Wait. A nurse will make you aware as soon as we know more." He nodded, then continued down the hallway.

My knees gave out, causing me to flop back in the chair. What was I supposed to do with that lack of information? I couldn't sit here anymore. I needed to move.

I left my phone number at the main desk, requesting them to call me if anything happened while I was gone. Leaving probably wasn't the right thing to do by my brother, but I had to figure out what the fuck had happened, and going back to the Plaza Towers felt like it was where I needed to be.

The heavy rock in my stomach seemed to double in size as my strides got longer. Taxi's lined the street, making one easy to grab.

My mind raced as we drove to the Towers. Maybe Jamie was hiding somewhere in the Tower, terrified to come out. Or maybe she was hurt, lying in a closet somewhere, slowly slipping away like Nathan.

Fuck. I had to get to her. Nathan was in good hands, and searching for her was my top priority.

Cop cars were everywhere when we finally reached the Towers. *Good, maybe they've found Jamie*. But deep down, I knew that likely wasn't true.

I slid under the yellow caution tape, speed walking to the elevator. 'Sir,' a deep voice commanded as I walked into the elevator. I ignored it. This was technically still my building, and they could go fuck themselves if they thought I wasn't allowed on the premises, cops or not.

The heavy-set officer began running toward me as the doors to the elevator closed. My lip twitched irritably while I watched him barely move fast enough to catch me. Not the shape an officer should be in, that's for sure.

The long ride to the top of the suite felt endless, and I let out a nervous breath once the elevator pinged. The doors slid open and my body was flung backward, my hands shooting in the air. A more physically fit cop was pointing a gun straight at my chest.

"Get down on the ground."

I did as he commanded. "I'm Mitch Conklin, the site manager for this building."

Two other officers swarmed the small space, one shoving his knee into my back causing me to lay face first on the concrete. He pulled my hands behind my head. I fought a grunt of pain from escaping my mouth. They meant business.

"No one's allowed in the building, owner or not. You failed to comply with an officer downstairs."

"He didn't say anything to me," I insisted. It was true, he just said, 'hey' because he was too winded to speak. "Please, I'm just trying to figure out what happened to my brother and—"

I paused when the cop shoved my cheek to the ground.

"Who's your brother?" a new voice that remained faceless asked.

My jaw dug into the ground. "Nathan Conklin. He was meeting the owner of the building with another associate. I came by about an hour ago and found him on the ground, barely alive. I called 911."

Silence passed, then the pressure pushing my head into the ground was released. "Bring him to Hendry." My arms were clamped together behind my back from the jumpy cop who was quick to tackle me.

"Is this necessary?" I muttered, flexing my wrists against his hold.

He glared at me, then gave a rough nudge in the middle of my back, forcing me to move forward. We walked through the penthouse, men in uniforms searching and examining every nook and crevice.

"Here's our intruder," the jackass holding my wrists said to a man standing in the room where I'd found Nathan earlier. "Says he's the brother of the man who was attacked here."

The man didn't acknowledge my presence but crouched next to the puddle of Nathan's blood. I swallowed hard, moving my eyes toward my feet to avoid the sight.

"Go watch the elevator, Slaydor."

My wrists were released, followed by an elbow shove. I turned and glared at him as he walked out of the room. *Fucker better watch himself.*

The man remained crouched, not moving his eyes from the ground. "So, why are you here, Mr. Conklin? Shouldn't you be at the hospital with your brother?"

I swallowed the lump in my throat. "Did you find anyone else here?"

He cocked his head in my direction. "You mean the perp? If we found him, Mr. Conklin, you'd be lying on this very floor next to your brother, both of you dead."

I scowled. "My brother didn't come here alone. He was with another employee." *The love of my life.*

"And how do you know that?"

My jaw ticked. "Because she's the reason I came here to begin with."

"Came here now?"

Was he an idiot? "No, came here when I found Nathan."

"How do you know she was coming with him?"

"Because she texted me."

He finally stood, walking toward me. He was in a navy suit, his short, dark hair slicked back with gel. Cool blue eyes took me in from head to toe, stopping on the large blood stain of my white T-shirt.

"Can I see the text?"

I pulled my phone out, scrolling to find the text before handing it to him.

"I have to meet with Nathan and Kobiashi at Plaza Towers. I won't be able to pick you up from the airport, frowny face. Call you when I'm done." He paused before he read the last sentence. "I can't wait to see you."

A slight flush crept up my neck when he spoke the last of the text. His eyes found mine, catching my reaction.

"More than a work associate?"

My gaze lowered to the floor. "Something like that." Even though I'd spilled my guts to Jamie before she came back to Miami, I had no idea what our title was.

He raised a brow in my direction.

I shook my head. "I don't know where she is. I'm worried something happened to her."

"Yes, but you don't know if she actually came here."

My temper was rising. "I just showed you the text."

"A text doesn't mean anything."

I ran my hand through my hair in frustration.

"Her phone was on the ground when I found Nathan," I added. "She originally called 911."

"Her phone isn't here now."

"That's because it's in my back pocket." I pulled it out, flashing it in front of his face.

"Why would you take it?"

"I don't know, I just did." I was beyond irritated at this point, and he wasn't answering any of my questions. "Who are you, anyway?"

He gave a half smile. "Detective Hendry." He held his hand out for me to shake. I eyed it, then took it. The way he gripped my hand was strong, and I could sense his power.

"The text said she was meeting with Nathan and Kobiashi. Who is Kobiashi?" Hendry let go of my hand and continued strolling around the room.

"He's the owner of this building. My company designed and built it for him. I assume that's why they were meeting here."

Then, I had an epiphany. "Here, I have Nathan's phone, too. I bet he has a text from Kobiashi."

Hendry squinted while I pulled out Nathan's phone from my other pocket. "Why do you have his phone?"

"I had to take everything off of him before they shocked him back to life with the defibrillator," I grumbled in frustration.

I searched Nathan's phone while Hendry looked over my shoulder. Sure enough, a text labeled *Biak Kobiashi2* came through at 10:37 a.m. telling Nathan to meet him at the penthouse.

"Grimson," Hendry yelled. Another officer appeared. "Please make contact with a Biak Kobiashi. I'd like to bring him in for questioning." The officer nodded, then took off into the other room.

"Do you think you could come down to the station tonight?" Hendry asked while walking out of the room as I followed.

"I guess. I mean, I need to go back to the hospital. But what about Jamie?"

"We can't file a missing person's report for another forty-eight hours."

My jaw dropped. "Don't you think under the circumstances the whole forty-eight hour thing should be forgiven?"

"That's the law, Mr. Conklin. We don't have any solid proof that she was even here."

"Are you fucking kidding me? You saw the text!"

"Sure, but that doesn't mean she wrote it."

My blood was boiling now. "She texted about Kobiashi. You were quick to set up an appointment with him."

He stopped in his tracks, turning to face me. We were in the kitchen now. "And I'm going to ask Mr. Kobiashi if he had a meeting with Nathan and this Jamie...?"

"Jamie Rae," I finished for him. "Some psycho tried to kill my brother. How do you know he didn't take Jamie with him?"

He took a step toward me, his eyebrows narrowing. "And how do I know she didn't park her car and walk down the road to the nearest coffee shop while Nathan went upstairs? Is her car even outside? Maybe Jamie and the Kobiashi guy left in his car somewhere, leaving Nathan behind, then he got attacked. There are so many possible scenarios. Maybe she just said she and Nathan were meeting there because they wanted to have a secret rendezvous and it happened to turn ugly?"

I bit the insides of my cheeks, then spoke in a low tone. "What are you implying?"

"I'm implying that I need more information, and I'm going to have to find that information before I spend taxpayer's money searching for an adult who might not be missing. Now, if you care about your brother, I'd suggest you go back to the hospital."

I took a deep breath, not wanting to lose my shit on this stupid detective. I wasn't going to wait for him to piece anything together. I needed to know what the hell was going on, and where Jamie was. I'd promised to take away her pain and protect her, and that was exactly what I planned to do.

"Grimson!" In a blink, the officer was by Hendry's side again. "Get Mr. Conklin's information for me so I can reach him."

I clenched my jaw as I took him in, then pulled out my card and handed it to Grimson. My mouth stayed shut in a firm line as I turned to go back to the hospital, but his voice stopped me before I reached the elevator.

"Mr. Conklin, we'll be in touch."

***

My head began to play games with me as I left my house after changing my blood stained shirt. Was Jamie with Nathan? Did she really get kidnapped? Or was I making this all up in my head? I was on auto pilot. Before I knew what was happening, I was in my car and traveling to Kobiashi's building. On the way, I passed a small diner in a strip mall. My eyes widened when I saw a white Lexus parked by a meter out front. I slammed on my breaks, nearly getting rear ended. That was Jamie's car. Maybe she was still at the diner? Waiting for Nathan?

I double parked next to her car but frowned when I glanced inside. There was a car seat. My hope fell. This wasn't Jamie's car. *But where was her car?* Was she in it somewhere? Maybe she was at home this whole time? She did say she hadn't been feeling well.

I sped to Kobiashi's building. I had to ask him what the fuck was going on, knowing most likely he was the reason for my brother's critical condition and Jamie's whereabouts.

Why are successful businessmen such shady fuckers? I knew Conklin had issues with drug deals on our properties, and I didn't help with that situation for a while, but we were clean now. Whatever happened in that penthouse was probably a deal gone wrong, and Nathan and Jamie were innocent bystanders.

My foot slammed on the break as soon as I reached his building, I jetted out of the car and through the double doors of the mile high building that was Kobiashi's headquarters. The moment I got to Kobiashi's office floor, I was stopped in my tracks by the detective.

"Mr. Conklin, didn't expect to see you here." His question was one of surprise, but he knew better.

"Something tells me that's not true."

He shrugged. "So maybe I had a hunch."

"I needed answers and you weren't giving them to me," I said firmly, walking past him to enter the reception hall.

"You should really let me do my job," Hendry said evenly, following me into the room.

Ignoring him, I greeted the receptionist who was talking to another woman. "I need to speak with Kobiashi," I demanded.

"Mr. Kobiashi is in a meeting right now. I'm afraid he won't be able to see you," the woman who talked to the receptionist said after patting her hair down and throwing me a smile. Normally, I'd turn on the charm at this point, but I wasn't interested.

"This is an emergency."

Her smile faltered slightly, then she looked through a tablet in her hand. "Well, he won't be finished for another—hey!"

I flew past her desk, ignoring her protests.

"This isn't the way to go about this," Hendry said calmly as he passed the woman and followed behind me.

I shoved an office door open. A long conference table was filled with men in suits, Kobiashi at the end. He stood, cocking his head at me quizzically.

"I need to talk to you," I said firmly, ignoring the onlookers.

"I'm in the middle of a meeting. Surely my assistant informed you." I couldn't read his expression, but the irritation in his voice was obvious.

"Yes, sir, but Mr. Conklin and his friend were persistent," an out of breath voice said from behind me. "I can call security if you'd like."

Kobiashi met my eyes without speaking a word, then saw Hendry holding up his badge. *Maybe having him here wasn't so bad after all.*

"There's an issue with your penthouse."

Kobiashi sighed, then fixed his suit coat. "No, security won't be necessary. I'm sorry, gentlemen, but we need to take a short break." Angry eyes filled the room, but they were all too afraid of Kobiashi to complain about his sudden pause. "Mr. Conklin, detective, please join me in my office." He motioned his hand to a door behind him, and we followed.

"What's the problem?" Kobiashi asked while closing his office door and taking a seat at his desk.

"Did you have a meeting with Nathan and Jamie this morning?"

He inhaled a deep breath as he sat down. "No, I've had back to back meetings since seven a.m. Now, what's wrong with the penthouse?"

"Nathan Conklin was attacked there this morning." Both of my hands pressed down on his desk. "I got a text from Jamie while I was on the plane this morning saying you wanted to meet with the two of them at Plaza Towers. So I took a taxi straight there, and found Nathan beat to hell and barely breathing in the master bedroom."

Kobiashi straightened his shoulders. "I'll say it again, I did not have a meeting with Nathan and Ms. Rae."

I ground my teeth while pulling Nathan's phone from my back pocket. "Then why does Nathan have a text message from you?"

He let out a deep breath, then stood. He looked at the phone before pressing his intercom. "Rachael, could you please come to my office." Ten seconds later the same angry woman entered the threshold of Kobiashi's office. She still looked pissed.

"I don't think she's as interested in you as before," Hendry murmured. My jaw clenched as I glared at him.

"Yes?" she asked, overly sweet.

"Can I see your company phone, please?" he asked, holding out his hand. Her face went white.

"Her phone?" I asked. "But the contact said--"

"Biak Kobiashi2. I assume the *two* represents my second assistant. Rachael, your phone, please." Kobiashi's patience was dwindling.

Her eyes began to get wet as the words started to spill. "I'm sorry, sir, but I misplaced it this morning. I was making calls while getting your coffee, but on my way back from the shop I couldn't find it. I called the coffee shop, but they hadn't found it either. I planned on going there during my lunch to re-trace my steps."

Hendry took a step toward Kobiashi's assistant. "Whoever attacked Nathan Conklin this morning likely stole your phone to lure him to the towers."

My stomach sank, knowing that same person stole Jamie, too.

CHAPTER TWELVE

Mitch

The walls in the waiting room felt like they were caving in with each passing minute. It had been three and a half hours since I came back from Kobiashi's building, and I still couldn't think straight. I knew I needed to be here with my brother, but my heart was screaming to go look for Jamie. But I didn't know where to start, and I didn't know how to go about finding her.

Maybe the detective was right. Maybe there was more to the story, and she was wandering and doing her own thing. Lord knows she does whatever the hell she wants and when she wants. Maybe I scared her and she could be on a plane to Australia for all I knew.

My stomach twisted in another knot, wishing she were here and tucked under my arm. Her comfort would help erase the uneasy feeling in my gut, and I'd know she was safe.

"Any news?" Tyler asked as he rushed down the hall. He looked put together in his expensive suit pants, button up shirt, and a silk tie, but his tired eyes with dark circles showed he was a mess inside. I was thankful he'd found a flight so quickly.

I stood, awkwardly reaching out to hug him. The flood of emotion got the best of me the moment I saw him. Tears threatened, and I wasn't sure how much longer I could hold them back. His arms wrapped around me, holding me close.

"What happened?" he whispered. Our embrace broke and we each took a seat.

"I found him at Kobiashi's new set of high rise condos. You know the Plaza Towers? Jamie sent me a text saying they were meeting Kobiashi." My hands found my head. "I had this bad feeling, so I took a cab there. When I got to the penthouse, he was lying in a puddle of blood." I choked on my words with the last part. Tyler put his hand on my shoulder, urging me to continue.

"He responded a little, but then he stopped breathing."

Tyler's hand gripped my shoulder tighter. Nathan and Tyler were extremely close. Tyler looked up to him more than he'd ever looked up to our father. I rubbed my face with both hands, attempting to stop my body from shaking.

"I had to give him CPR. I didn't know if..."

Tyler pulled me into a side hug, his head pressed to mine. "Mitch, you obviously saved his life. You did everything right. We wouldn't be sitting in this waiting room if you hadn't thought so quickly on your feet."

I licked a salty tear from my lips. "The AED saved his life, not me. Took five shocks before he started breathing again. It was the longest few minutes of my life."

"I can imagine." He lifted his head, searching the room. "Where's Jamie? Is she back at the office? I figured she'd be here."

Letting out a huge breath of air, I lifted my head so I could look at him. "I don't know," I whispered. "I think whoever attacked Nathan took her."

Tears fell as my head found Tyler's shoulder. Both his arms caged me. "We'll find her. Nathan will be okay. This is all going to work out. We've been through so much as a family, I think we can handle this. Maybe Becca could call Jamie's family and see if they've heard from her? Do you know for sure she was with Nathan?"

My jaw ticked. He sounded like that pain in the ass detective. "Her phone was laying next to Nathan when I found him. She called 911, then disappeared."

Tyler sighed, taking one arm off of me to rub his face. "You'd think after all the shit we dealt with in Grand Rapids we'd catch a break."

I chuckled under my breath in agreement.

Tyler stood. "Let's go grab something to eat. I'll call Becca while you call Mom?" My brow rose at him. "Fine. I'll call mom. Come on."

"I'm not hungry."

"Me either, but it'll give us something to do while we wait."

Walking through the white hallway of the hospital was nerve-wracking. I jumped every time I heard a page over the loud speaker, paranoid I'd hear that chilling 'code blue.' Once we got our mugs and a few pastries to pick at from the cafeteria, Tyler paced the entrance while making the necessary calls. I knew Mom would likely be pissed I hadn't call her sooner, but I didn't have the balls to hear her shed tears.

My coffee was warm between my hands, the first sip slightly burning my tongue. The black coffee reminded me of Jamie. She always loaded her cup with flavored creamer. The thought made my lip quirk, remembering her cuddled under my sheets and giving me crap for not having anything flavored in my fridge. The scent brought me a smudge of comfort, remembering the color I'd brought out in her cheeks before making the coffee that morning.

Yawning, I took another sip to help keep me awake. Although the memory of Jamie warmed my heart momentarily, visions of Jamie being taken played in my mind when I blinked, killing those pleasant feelings, and I could only imagine how horrifying my dreams were going to be.

"Becca's catching an early flight tomorrow morning, and Mom will be here later in the day." Tyler sat down across from me. "She said she'd call Jamie's parents. So did something happen between the two of you?"

I nodded twice, squinting my eyes while I bit my lip. Why was this so hard? My heart bled for this woman, and I was willing to search the continent until I found her, yet it was so difficult to open up about how she made me feel.

Tyler readjusted himself in his seat. "Look, I know you've been fixated on her, and she might seem like a challenge—"

"It's not like that," I fired at him, frustrated with his patronizing tone. "I've never felt this way about a woman."

Tyler's eyes filled with pity. "Becca says Jamie's never had a long term relationship if any relationship at all."

"Neither have I. I'm... I'm in love with her."

Tyler's jaw dropped. "Does she know this?"

"Yes," I choked out.

"Does she feel the same way?"

The lump in my throat was thick as I swallowed. I'd told her how I felt, that I wanted more with her, that she boggled me in the most extraordinary way, and that I loved her. But she didn't say anything back. Her kiss, though... That spoke volumes. I thought maybe she was just stunned by my declaration. I did pull those three delicate words out of left field. We'd only been intimate a few times, but I'd submitted to her long before. And she knew she had me in the palms of her hands.

"Mitch?" Tyler pulled me from my thoughts.

"She didn't exactly say it. It's different. She doesn't open up easily. She's got this mile high wall. But I think she wants me to break it down. She's vulnerable with me."

Tyler sighed. "She's really got you baffled, doesn't she?"

"Jamie's the only woman I've stripped myself completely bare for, changed my ways and devoted my life to. She's shifted my entire world, and I won't be able to stand upright again until she's safe in my arms."

Tyler's skepticism turned into a smirk. "That was poetic. You really did fall in love."

I slouched in my chair, taking another sip of my coffee. "Like the tears from a Greek goddess."

"Huh?"

I closed my eyes, not wanting to explain my secret obsession with the stars and the myths behind them. As of now, my brothers thought I was an idiot, not an astronomy scholar.

Tyler's phone buzzed. "Hey … No word? … Okay, call me before you go to bed. … Love you too." Tyler hung up the phone, then studied me before he spoke. "Jamie's parents haven't heard from her."

My heart sank even though I already knew that answer. Jamie was in trouble, and I had no clue how to save her. Where do I even start? I couldn't just sit around while she was missing, but I couldn't leave Nathan either. I felt like God was playing tug-of-war with my heart.

"Have you talked to the police yet?"

"Yeah. The detective seems like a real winner," I chided. "Told me he was going to wait forty-eight hours to file a missing person's report. He's still waiting even though he figured out Nathan and Jamie were set up to be in that penthouse," I grumbled.

My phone buzzed as I shifted in my seat. A smidgen of hope fluttered in my stomach when I saw it was an unknown number. "Hello?" I answered quickly, my voice jumping an octave in anticipation.

"Mitch? Hi, this is Leslie, Jamie's mom."

Her voice shook, causing my tongue to catch in my throat. "Hi, Leslie."

"I just talked to Becca, Jamie's best friend. She gave me your phone number. I hope that's okay."

I nodded as though she could see me. "Of course." The quiet fuzz over the phone was killing me. I didn't know what to say to her because my thoughts on what happened might terrify her more than they terrified me.

"Is something going on with her? Becca said your brother was... attacked. Then she asked me if I'd spoken to Jamie at all today."

I stood. Tyler furrowed his brows, but I held up my finger insinuating I'd be back in a minute before I walked into the hall. "Yeah, he's in the hospital now. I'm waiting for him to get out of surgery."

"Oh, I'm so sorry. I didn't realize it was that serious." Her voice shook even more than before. She was worried about her daughter, but too afraid to ask.

I took a deep breath, then spilled. "Jamie texted me that she was going to be with Nathan this morning, but when I found Nathan, she wasn't with him." My hand began to shake while I tried to push the next sentence out of my mouth. "Her phone was on the ground next to him. She called 911."

"What are you trying to say?"

I took another deep breath. "I think whoever attacked my brother might have taken Jamie."

Her mother gasped into the phone. "Took her? Who would take my baby?" I closed my eyes, wondering the same thing. "Do the police know? What do we do? I need to do something!"

"Yes, the police are involved. I talked to the detective myself."

Leslie began to weep over the phone. Soon the chattering of Jamie's younger siblings filtered over her mother's quiet sobs, and I could tell she was trying to get herself together.

"I'll call you as soon as I know more, okay? If you want, you can stay at Jamie's condo. I have a key." I knew her family struggled, and as much as I wanted to wrap myself in Jamie's sheets tonight, her parents needed that comfort as bad as I did.

"Thank you, but I need to figure out what to do with Jamie's siblings and talk to Ryan. Call me if you hear something?"

"Of course."

As I hung up the phone, Tyler began walking toward me. "Jamie's parents?"

"Yeah. That was almost as difficult as when I called you this morning." I sunk to the ground, leaning my elbows on my knees and resting my head on my forearms. Tyler slid down the wall to sit as well.

"You had me worried as hell. I expected Nathan's voice, not yours."

"I didn't know what the fuck to do. I still don't know what to do," I admitted to Tyler.

"I think it's out of our hands at this point."

We shared glances, our fears written on each of our faces. As if we needed sound to solidify our fears, a code blue was announced for Nathan's floor. Doctors flew past us as we both jumped to our feet, moving in unison.

"You don't think..."

Tyler shook his head. "I doubt they'd announce that for someone in surgery."

Our paces picked up, both of us terrified it was Nathan's body that had crashed. We flew into the waiting room, nearly knocking over a woman dressed from head to toe in scrubs.

"Are you the family of Nathan Conklin?"

Tyler and I nodded.

She smiled slightly. "Hi, my name is Amanda. I'm one of the hospital's social workers. Can you both come with me?"

My heart beat faster with every step, my eyes glancing at Tyler every few paces. Was this where she told us Nathan didn't make it through surgery?

Amanda opened a door to a small office with a desk and a few chairs. "Please, have a seat." Tyler sat right away, his hands making a steeple under his chin as he waited patiently.

I didn't have his patience.

"Is Nathan okay?" I blurted, my body tense as I clutched the back of one of the chairs with white knuckles.

She and Tyler turned to look in my direction. His smile was gone. "We were able to stop the internal bleeding. Besides a few broken ribs and lacerations to his face, the majority of his problems were from the knife wound in his lower left abdomen."

Tyler nodded toward my chair for me to sit, so I did, my leg bouncing in anticipation. She got situated in her seat, then looked at the two of us.

"Nathan's body has withstood a great deal of trauma within the past twelve hours. He lost over two liters of blood and his brain has suffered from the loss of oxygen. His body has reacted—"

"Reacted?" Tyler asked.

"He's in a coma. It's very typical for a patient's body to fall into a coma after they've suffered from cardiac arrest, especially since Nathan wasn't breathing for nearly five minutes."

My mind was reeling. "So what does that mean, though? How long will he be in a coma?"

"We don't know. Could be a few days or even months."

"You said loss of oxygen. Does that mean his brain is… damaged?" Tyler's voice cracked. *When* Nathan woke up, he could be brain dead.

Amanda rested both hands on the desk between us. "We will monitor his brain activity, but won't know for sure until he comes out of the coma."

Tyler's head fell into his hands as my body shook. For the first time, it wasn't from fear or sorrow, but from anger. I wanted to kill the fucker who beat my brother so badly that he wouldn't wake up. My fist slammed down on the table as I shot out of my chair, finding the exit.

"Where are you going?" Tyler commanded. "Excuse me a moment," he murmured to her as he stood to follow me.

"Mitch, stop."

I paused in my tracks, pounding my fists against the wall. "I can't just sit here."

"We've been waiting all day for answers, and that woman is giving them to us. Now be a man and get back in there."

"She didn't give us an answer. They have no idea what the fuck is going on until he wakes up."

"And she may have more to say. I know you're angry right now, but that's not going to solve anything. You think I don't want to go find the asshole who did this? Because trust me, I want to strangle him with my own two hands. But we can't do that. Nathan needs us."

Hatred filled me for Nathan's attacker, but also for myself. If I'd come in the night before, or taken an earlier flight, I would have been there with them. If I'd had a car at the airport, I could have sped to the building and gotten there earlier, maybe even in the middle of the assault.

And Jamie...

My forehead rested against the back of my clenched fists, tears running down my cheeks and onto the floor. I needed her, and the sick feeling in my gut told me she needed me a thousand times more.

Tyler pulled me to him, hugging me with all his strength. "Let's go back in there. Then maybe we can see Nathan."

As we turned, Amanda was standing in the hall staring at us. I shrugged away from his embrace. "Let's meet tomorrow morning. I'm sure you'll have more questions by then. Would you like to see Nathan now?"

"Yes," we said in unison.

"Follow me. He's cleaned up and bandaged, but please try not to let all the wires and medical equipment scare you. They're there to keep him alive and to help him recover."

I nodded, knowing no matter what Nathan was hooked up to, he wouldn't look as horrible as he had when he'd stopped breathing.

The hallways felt bare and rigid, the walls too white and clean. I looked down at my hands, seeing dried blood underneath my nails from earlier in the day, feeling dirtier than I'd ever felt. The dryness formed in my throat, the buzz of the fluorescent lights making each step achingly painful. The anticipation was overwhelming, and I couldn't shake my unsteady nerves.

Turning down another hall, Tyler placed his hand on my shoulder, stepping in stride with me. The way his fingers drummed methodically on my shoulder gave away that he was just as anxious. We'd already lost our father. Nathan was the next closest to filling those shoes.

"Here we are," she said quietly.

We both paused before crossing the threshold of the room, terrified to see our eldest brother hanging by a thread. Tyler nodded for me to step forward, and I did, my eyes searching the room to find Nathan.

He was covered in tubes, his face swollen with bruises and scrapes. His skin ghostly white, no sign of emotion or pain straining his features. He was always so strong, so mischievous, but the grin we all shared was gone, only a beat up shell surrounding him. It tore at my heart to see him so wrecked.

Tyler cautiously pulled a chair over so he could sit beside Nathan's bed. His elbows rested on his knees, his hands holding his head while he examined him. Tyler's eyes were big and concerned.

"He can't feel anything, right?" I asked, standing next to Tyler.

"No, he's not conscious," she replied, standing at the end of the bed. "Though they say a loved one's voice can sometimes help to heal. You can touch him," she added after seeing Tyler's hand tentatively reached out to touch Nathan's forearm. Tyler's body shuddered in anticipation as he grazed Nathan's arm. My hand grasped his shoulder, wanting to soothe his fear.

"He's so cold," he whispered, moving his hand along Nathan's forearm.

"I can adjust the thermostat," she said, moving to the other side of the room. "A nurse will be in every half hour to take his vitals. I promise we'll take good care of him."

I nodded, turning to look at her. "Thank you. Could you give us a moment?" She smiled understandingly, then walked back to the hallway.

"You all right?" I asked Tyler, my hand patting his shoulder.

He didn't respond. One thing about Tyler, he didn't like to show his feelings, happy or sad. He was very private and kept to himself. I think Becca had started to thaw him, though. I'd noticed his eyes get wet a few times during Dad's funeral, and they hated each other.

The monitors continued to beep while Tyler and I sat and stared at our miracle of a brother. The buzz of my phone pulled me from my gaze on Nathan. Not wanting to disturb Tyler, I walked into the hall, answering my phone without looking at the number.

"Mitch, it's Detective Hendry. I'd like to meet with you tomorrow morning at my station if possible." His tone was clipped and rubbed me the wrong way. "I'd like to talk more about your brother."

"And Jamie," I added. "What's the next step to find her?"

"We'll talk more tomorrow."

I tried to hold back my frustration. "Fine."

"I'll text you with a time." He hung up without saying goodbye.

Shoving the phone back in my pocket, I peeked into Nathan's room. Tyler's lips were moving as though he was talking to Nathan. They always had a special bond that didn't include me. Maybe it was because I was the youngest or because I didn't share the same interests as them. They were businessmen while I needed to use my hands. They thought out their lives, and I flew by the seat of my pants. They were committed to people and work, and I was committed only to myself.

But not anymore…

I'd expressed my love for Jamie, practically ripping my heart out and handing it to her, taking the chance that she'd either stomp on it or cherish it forever.

I had to find her. She was my saving grace, and there was no way she was going to slip through my fingers. No one was going to take her from me, that was for damn sure.

I left Tyler without saying goodbye. I'd send him a text once I got to my car. I needed to search for Jamie, and the best place for me to start was where she last was, tracing her steps. Tonight, I'd go to her condo, charge her phone, and look through her stuff. That aching feeling in my chest said she needed me to search every nook and crevice until I found answers.

***

The air was sticky and damp by the time I reached Jamie's condo. I'd taken Nathan's key, a pang of jealousy spreading through me knowing he'd shared space with the woman I loved.

Walking up the small flight of stairs was an eerie feeling. What if she were inside sleeping? She did say she hadn't been feeling well. My spirits lifted, thoughts of her zonked out on the couch, sleeping soundly. *I never thought I'd want her to be sick.* But her car wasn't here and most likely she wouldn't be either.

I turned the knob quickly, opening the door and searching for the light switch. I couldn't contain the warmth I felt once I entered her space. The décor was minimal, but it felt so much like Jamie. The main wall was painted a warm red, with cool grays on the others, and a few abstract photos of bodies dancing freely were placed on the main wall in the living room. Cream-colored furnishings filled the space.

A photo of her, Becca, Tyler, and Nathan sat on an end table. I reached for it, bringing it closer to my face so I could examine it. My heart beat raced seeing her glowing with happiness. I set the photo back down, remembering why I was here in the first place. The condo wasn't very big, so finding Jamie's room would be easy. My spirits faded when I searched all but one room. Sure enough, only an empty queen size bed was in the center of the room when I flipped on the light.

I puffed out a breath of air. She really wasn't here and it was dumb of me to think so. There were too many signs pointing in bad directions. I ran my fingers along the sheets of the empty bed, closing my eyes and imagining her lying cozy and safe under the blankets where I could crawl under the sheets with her.

Before I knew what I was doing, I slid into the coolness of her sheets. My arms instantly reached for her pillow, burrowing my face into the down-feathered fabric. It smelled like her, citrus and clean, making me long for the real Jamie. Exhaustion overcame me as I daydreamed about holding her. Feeling her back against my chest and inhaling her scent would be soothing after all that had happened today. Kissing her ear or the nape of her neck, making a sweet giggle escape those plush lips would put me on cloud nine. But she wasn't here, and I had no idea when the next time I'd see her again would be.

Sleeping four hours straight without any nightmares was a miracle after all of the trauma. I sprung out of Jamie's bed, rubbing my face frantically to wake up, only to realize she was still gone.

My phone buzzed in my pocket.

Still no change. Try to get some sleep.

I tossed my phone on the bed, putting my head in my hands and attempting to gain my thoughts. I hadn't meant to fall asleep so quickly last night, and I needed to figure out a game plan. First, I needed to search for *something*.

I'd always gotten the feeling Jamie wasn't telling me the entire truth about her. She was so private, putting up walls that I thought I was starting to break down. But there was no doubt something devastating had happened in her past.

There was the death of her brother, which had obviously affected her. But there was something more. Another reason why she had trouble getting close to me. Why she didn't like her neck touched or why, when I tried to go behind her, she froze as though she'd fallen into a dark hole and couldn't get back out.

"All right, Jamie Rae. Forgive me for what I'm about to do."

I was on my feet, opening her clothing drawers. Of course, I came across her underwear drawer first. I was already supporting a halfie from waking up, and seeing her lacy undergarments wasn't helping the blood to even out. Imagining her perfect ass in the deep-red lacy thong made all kinds of filthy fantasies pop into my head.

Stop it.

I threw the lacy demon back, searching more frantically. Nothing seemed suspicious in her drawers, so I moved to the closet. Jesus, she was organized. Every dress was color coordinated and hanging nicely, matching heels lined underneath. The woman could wear a sack and look beautiful, but I couldn't help but examine a few of the dresses, remembering some of them that had made my chase for her to say yes to going out on a date all the more exciting.

Calm the fuck down. At this rate, I was going to be jerking off in her closet like a fucking psycho.

I stepped out of her closet, then headed for her bathroom, rummaging through the medicine cabinet. Nothing interesting there, only girly shit, so I got on my knees, looking underneath the bed and desk. Nothing. Her desk only held a few finance things, which meant shit to me. Numbers only gave me a headache. My heart tugged, remembering the app she'd searched so hard to create to help me with my dyscalculia.

She cared. There's no way she was avoiding me this time.

Finally, I came to the drawer by her bed. It stuck at first, but with a good yank, it came open. A few candles, magazines, an eReader, some pictures and...

I smirked. *Naughty girl.* My thumb found the button on the vibrator, my brows raising with the strength. I shut it off and held it between my legs. My cock was way bigger than this, and I was sure I'd made her come harder than this piece of rubber.

The vibrator got tossed back in the drawer as I fumbled through more stuff. Just when I was about to lose my mind and sanity, I pulled out a thick, unmarked manila envelope. Standing over her bed, I opened it, spilling its contents. My eyes widened as thick black carbon papers covered her dark red bedspread. They were all folded twice with the same wax seal. The tremor that went through my arm traveled through my body as I reached for one. Her name was in white ink, and the message inside was short and to the point. The air whooshed from my chest as though I'd been hit by a baseball bat.

Jamie was being stalked.

CHAPTER THIRTEEN

Mitch

Now you're getting it. Remember who's good for you.
Wear those stockings more often.
-Rod

My face paled with each letter I read. Some threatening, some passionate, but they were all freaky as fuck. Whoever wrote these letters desired Jamie, and had been watching her for a very long time. There were hundreds of them.

How could she keep this a secret from me? Protecting her from this creep would have been my number one priority. Maybe this was why she was so guarded? My head spun as I sat down on her bed amongst the letters. *What the fuck was going on?*

Suddenly, the sound of the front door creaked open, followed by murmured voices trailing down the hall. A tiny hint of hope emerged but was squashed when I realized it was Becca and Tyler.

Becca appeared at Jamie's bedroom door. "Oh hey, Mitch. How are you doing?" Her voice was somber as she took a cautious step toward me, reaching her arms out to hug me.

I stayed put, declining her invitation. I needed answers. "Did you know about these?"

Her brows furrowed as she stared at me. "About what?"

My jaw was clenched tight as I held up one of the black letters. "These. You know, the hundreds of creepy letters I just found in Jamie's drawer."

Becca frowned as she stepped past me, grabbing one of the letters from the bed. "I've never seen anything like this." Tyler walked behind her, his focus on the piles of letters on the bed.

"What do you mean you *haven't* seen any of these? Weren't you roommates?"

Becca's frown deepened. "Yes, but it doesn't mean I opened her mail."

My jaw ticked as I paced Jamie's room. "Well, whoever wrote these letters is dangerous."

"Who's Rod?" Tyler asked as he picked up one of the letters.

"I've never heard her mention a Rod," Becca whispered, her mind reeling as her eyes searched the letters.

"Whoever this Rod guy is, he's responsible for Nathan and has Jamie. She's in trouble." My hands shook as I began to shove the letters back into the large manila envelope where I found them.

"What do you mean?" Becca's voice shook. "You think someone took Jamie?"

"I think that's fucking obvious," I snapped. A tear fell from Becca's eye, but I didn't care. "You haven't heard from her, and neither have I. She was with Nathan, and he got beat nearly to death. Did you ever notice any signs? Any weird ex-boyfriends?"

Becca shook her head, causing me to lose my cool. "How could you not have known about this? I thought you were Jamie's best friend!" I shouted, my hands thrown to my sides in frustration.

Becca narrowed her eyes. "She *is* my best friend. But she's also extremely private. I assumed you'd figured that out by now."

I waved the envelope in the air. "Some things aren't meant to be kept private."

"Calm down," Tyler demanded as he slid in front of Becca protectively.

"Calm down? How am I supposed to calm down? My brother's in a coma in the hospital and the woman I'm in love with has been kidnapped and no one seems to have any answers! Maybe if your wife were a better friend—"

"Excuse me?" Becca blurted, shoving Tyler to the side and going toe to toe with me. "Besides Nathan, I'm the only friend Jamie has. Just because she didn't open up to me about these letters doesn't mean I don't care about her."

"Well, maybe if you were more observant, you'd have realized she was so private because of these," I hissed, waving a handful of letters in her face.

Tyler firmly placed his hand on my shoulder, pulling me back from his wife. "We need to take these letters to the police. For all we know, Jamie could already have a restraining order against someone."

I shrugged from Tyler's grasp and strode toward the door.

"Mitch, where are you going?" Tyler asked in frustration.

"To figure out who the hell this Rod guy is and to get Jamie."

***

I couldn't drive around searching for Jamie. All of these letters scattered on my passenger seat felt like a ticking time bomb. For all I knew someone was torturing her, touching her...

A chill flew up my spine, and my foot laid heavier on the gas.

Rod... Rod... Rod...

The name kept flashing like a neon sign in my head. I didn't know any Rods, and I'd never heard Jamie say the name.

Pulling up to the police station, I didn't even bother putting coins in the meter. The ticket would be worth it if it meant getting this valuable piece of information to Hendry as soon as possible. I was going to be early for Hendry's meeting.

The building was big with people shuffling every which way, and I was taken aback by how active the place was. My gaze finally set on the receptionist. Two big men in suits were standing next to the glass window the woman worked behind. I recognized them from yesterday in Plaza Towers.

"I have an appointment with Detective Hendry."

"Name?"

"Mitch Conklin."

She typed on a computer for a few moments, her eyes never leaving the screen. "You're not scheduled for another hour. You can either wait or come back."

"But it's important. I have information regarding Jamie Rae. She's in serious danger," I pleaded.

The two officers stopped talking and looked at me. "Want me to get Hendry?" one of them asked.

She shook her head in annoyance. "Detective Hendry isn't in yet. You'll have to wait—"

"But this is an import—"

A large hand squeezed my shoulder. "The lady said he's not here and you have to wait. Is there going to be a problem?" one of the officers asked.

If he thought he was going to intimidate me, he was wrong. I spun to face him, shrugging his hand off my shoulder in the process. "I have information that could save this woman's life. She's in danger, and something needs to be done. Get a hold of him," I demanded, stepping close so I was in his space.

That was a bad idea.

He grabbed my wrist, and in one swift motion, my whole body turned so I was flat on my stomach, my arm pinned uncomfortably behind my back with a knee settled between my shoulder blades. My head was slammed against the ground with his other free hand. I could barely breathe from the crushing weight on my head and back.

While one cop held me down, the other squatted next to me. "Listen, you little prick, you don't tell us what to do. Where we come from, we treat people with respect."

"So when we find Jamie Rae dead, I'll blame you," I spat through sporadic breaths. The knee drove harder into my back, causing me to grunt in pain.

"I don't think that's necessary, gentlemen."

I glanced up, noticing Hendry above me with amusement on his face. He held a folder in one hand and a travel coffee mug in the other. Both men chuckled, then the pressure on my back released.

"How's it going, Detective?"

"Another lovely morning. Mr. Conklin, eager for our visit?"

I stood instantly. The glare I threw toward both cops didn't go unnoticed by Hendry. He gave me a smirk.

"I'd watch your mouth around these two. Especially Slaydor. They're always looking for trouble. Follow me to my office."

Both officers' lips twitched in agreement, their eyes never leaving me as I followed Hendry to his office.

"Not sure I deserved it that time," I muttered. Hendry laughed under his breath as he held a door open. I stopped in front of him and looked in the room. Only a table with a recorder was there with mirrors. I scowled. "This doesn't look like an office."

Hendry shrugged his shoulders. "This is my office today."

I swallowed. "Looks like an interrogation room."

"Is that what you think I'm going to do to you?"

I bit the inside of my cheek and walked past him, taking a seat at the empty table. Hendry took his time, placing the folder on the table and settling himself into the chair across from me. He fiddled with the recorder as he spoke.

"How's your brother?"

"Stable." I didn't want to talk about Nathan to this guy. It wasn't any of his business. I only wanted him to find out who put Nathan in the hospital. "I found these in Jamie's room," I said quickly, throwing the envelope on top of his folder. He glared at me, then took the envelope and examined it.

I nodded, encouraging him to dump out the contents. Just as I had done earlier on Jamie's bed, Hendry sprawled the letters on the table. His expression was unreadable as he saw the black letters thrown across the table. He rubbed his forehead while leaning back in his chair.

"Did you touch them?"

My stomach dropped. "Yes."

He bounced his leg for a moment while thinking, then leaned over the table, taking the manila envelope to move one of the letters so he could read it.

"They're all written the same way, from the same person."

"I see that. I'll have to send them for diagnostics. I'm going to guess we'll only find Jamie's, and now your prints, though. Normally perpetrators who go to this level take precautions when it comes to leaving their tracks. To be honest, you're lucky you found them."

"What do you mean?"

He moved the papers around now with the back of his pen. "I mean this 'Rod' character will probably come looking for them." He reached for his phone from the inside of his jacket, revealing his piece while doing so. "I need a surveillance crew twenty-four seven at the Acqualia Condominiums, specifically condo #239 on Sunnybrook." He hung up.

"How do you know where Jamie lives?"

Hendry moved a few papers around. "I'm a detective. I do my prep work."

I ran my hands over my face rapidly, both knees bouncing. "Please tell me this will help because I can't take this. We have to find her. This Rod person is obviously crazily obsessed."

Hendry's eyes darted from the letters to me, then back to me. "Did you write these letters?"

My jaw dropped. "Of course not."

He stared for a moment. "I had to ask. Has she ever talked about Rod?"

"No, I've never heard her talk about anyone with that name."

"How much do you really know about Jamie Rae?"

I blinked at him, feeling ashamed I was in love with a woman I really didn't know. "I might not know names, but I know someone's hurt her before."

Hendry raised a brow. "Please, explain."

The air felt thick as I squirmed in my seat. "I can just tell someone hurt her on a damaging level."

"Give me an example of how you can *tell.*"

"It's personal," I muttered.

Hendry squinted his eyes. "Mr. Conklin, do you want to find your friend?"

I swallowed. "She's my girlfriend," I corrected. "Well, we were heading in that direction."

"Okay, do you want to find your *girlfriend*?" I nodded. "Then I'll ask you again. How can you tell someone has hurt her?"

I shuffled in my seat again. "She doesn't like her neck to be touched."

Hendry scrunched his eyebrows in confusion.

"I mean, she clams up, goes to a completely different place if her neck gets touched."

"PTS?"

"I guess? She hasn't opened up to me about it yet."

"Anything else?"

I stared at my hands. Telling him about how she froze and mentally fell off the face of the earth when I went to have sex with her from behind didn't feel like information I needed to share. That wouldn't help figure this out. *Unless...*

"Do you think she knew him from before?"

Hendry's head quirked questioningly.

"Rod, the guy who wrote these letters. Do you think she could have had a relationship with him in some way?"

"Stalkers don't normally have real relationships with their victims. It's a fantasy inside their heads. Do you remember someone by the name of Rod now?"

I shook my head. "Just curious."

"There's always a possibility. I'll have to contact her family and friends. What else can you tell me about her?"

"She works for my family's company as the marketing coordinator. She stays in Miami most of the time but sometimes bounces to Grand Rapids. Basically, wherever Nathan needs her."

"What type of relationship did she have with Nathan Conklin?"

I sat back further in my chair, surprised by his question. "He's her boss."

Hendry shrugged his shoulders. "Just co-workers? Friends? Lovers?"

My whole body tensed. I was always jealous of their relationship. "They were friends as well."

He cocked his head to the side. "You didn't like that?"

"That they were friends? Why would that bother me?"

"Because your hands are in fists like you want to punch a hole in the table." My eyes found my hands, instantly flattening them on the cool metal.

"I want to be as close to Jamie as Nathan is," I confessed.

He moved his lips to the side as he thought. "So they were close."

"They are roommates whenever Nathan is in Miami." It was hard to share that information when I wanted to be Jamie's new roommate.

"So they stay in the same place. Different rooms?"

"Of course," I snorted. "Nathan isn't interested in her romantically."

He tilted his head in the other direction. "You sound jealous."

"I just told you I want to be closer to Jamie."

"Would you do anything to be close to her?"

I leaned forward on the table, looking him dead in the eye. "Jamie and I have been romantic, and I have strong feelings for her. I crave to build an unbreakable friendship to go along with our physical chemistry. So, yes, I would do anything to be close to her."

"Would you kill your own brother?"

My jaw dropped, almost hitting the table. "*What?*"

He shrugged his shoulders. "Would you write her letters? Wanting her to know you'd do anything for her?"

I flew to my feet, leaning over the table and pointing a finger in his direction. "Are you fucking crazy? Of course I'd never kill my brother. I fucking called 911, gave him CPR, pressed against his wound to stop his blood with my bare hands. I saved my brother's life," I hissed. "You're looking in the wrong places, and you're wasting valuable time. This Rod guy is fucking crazy, and YOU need to find him before he hurts Jamie!"

Hendry smiled while crossing his hands over one another in his lap. "I know you didn't try to kill your brother, Mr. Conklin. I've seen footage from the surveillance cameras at the airport. Doesn't mean you're in the clear, but your little tantrum just now might help. Please, sit back down."

I huffed out air, feeling extra tense.

"I pulled Jamie's file last night."

I furrowed my brows. "She has a file?"

Hendry laughed under his breath, setting the folder he'd brought in on top of the letters. "Quite a big one, actually."

I tilted my head, trying to get a glimpse at the now opened folder.

"Did you know she had a brother?"

"She has four. Well, I know one died in the Airforce. The others still live with her parents."

"Is that what she told you?"

I nodded. "Yeah, I've met them."

Hendry shook his head, throwing a file in front of me so I could see it better. "Her brother died in a car accident. Jamie was driving. Her blood alcohol level was fine, but she tested positive for marijuana. She was under the influence."

"What?" No wonder her brother's death seemed to cut so deep. "She only mentioned he died in his uniform, I just assumed..."

Hendry pointed to a spot on the paper. "The other driver was under the influence as well. He actually died of a cocaine overdose. Amazingly, he made it to the car with how much was found in his system. The car hit the passenger side, knocking them against a tree. They were trapped for almost four hours on a back road before another car came along. It was Jamie's prom night, assumed they were coming home from a party. She was coherent when found. She watched her brother slowly bleed out from being crushed."

My hand covered my mouth. Poor Jamie. Why hadn't she told me?

"She was on probation for two years. Lucky she didn't get charged with manslaughter. They let her off easy if you ask me. Probably helped that her father used to work for the force."

"What does this have to do with anything? So she had a tragedy happen, what, seven years ago? How is that going to help us find her?"

"Even though she was declared a victim in the case, the family of the other deceased driver might still have a grudge. He was supposedly her brother's best friend. I guess he and Jamie had a 'thing' and that's why Jamie and her brother left the party. Caused a big scene in front of the other party goers, so the report says."

I closed my eyes. I didn't like thinking about Jamie with other men.

Hendry stood, collecting the reports he'd laid in front of me and placing them back in the folder, leaving the black letters on the table. "I've asked enough questions for now."

"What now?" I asked curiously.

"I have a lot to do to help find who attacked your brother and maybe Jamie."

I left my chair and followed him. "What can I do?"

Hendry stopped and turned to me. "Stay out of the way and let me do my job. I'll make an official statement this evening after I've talked to a few more people. I can only hold off the press for so long."

"There has to be more. We have to—"

Hendry held his hands up to me. "*We don't do anything. I do.* Like I said, let me do my job, Mr. Conklin. I may look young, but I guarantee I know what I'm doing. Don't get in the way." His eyes blazed momentarily as if to intimidate me but then softened. "If you think of anything else that might be important, call me."

I nodded. Hendry was hopefully telling the truth, but his attitude rubbed me the wrong way. Wouldn't he want someone who knew Jamie to help him out? Then again, I guess I didn't know her that well. She may have opened up to me about her brother dying, but she didn't admit it was because she was driving under the influence and got into an accident. She'd made it sound like he died in combat.

"I'll walk you out," Hendry said as I stood there dumbfounded. "Try not to think of the worst case scenario," Hendry added while tapping his hand on my shoulder.

My doubts were killing me, though. What if she really took off because of me? I closed my eyes. That just couldn't be the case. She'd never leave Nathan like that.

Jamie's parents were sitting in the waiting room. "Mitch! It's so good to see you." Leslie leaped from her seat, wrapping her arms around me. "My mind won't stop spinning." Her voice quivered as she talked. I knew the feeling. My hand patted her back gently as she trembled.

"Any news?" Jamie's father asked as I peered at him over Leslie's shoulder.

Leslie let go of me, then huddled next to Ryan. "It's not like Jamie to just disappear. She's always kept good contact with us."

I swallowed the thick lump in my throat as my eyes found my feet. I couldn't face them. Part of being in a relationship with someone is protecting them, and I felt like I'd failed at that crucial part of being in love.

"Mr. and Mrs. Rae, I assume?" Hendry asked while holding out his hand.

"Yes, don't I know you?" Ryan asked while furrowing his eyebrows.

Hendry smiled and nodded. "I was a cadet at your shop in Point Canal."

A small grin appeared on Ryan's face. I'd forgotten he used to be a sheriff. No wonder he was chatting it up with those two goons. Ryan probably knew most of the police officers here. Point Canal wasn't that far away from South Beach. "That's right. Looks like you've moved up in the ranking."

Hendry nodded with the same grin on his face. "Guess I did something right. Would you like to come to my office?"

Both of Jamie's parents nodded. Leslie rubbed my bicep as she walked by. "I'll call you when we're done?"

"Please do." I waved as they followed Hendry.

"Wow, you had a thing with Sheriff Rae's daughter?" one of the officers who'd jumped me asked.

I rolled my eyes in his direction. "I *have* a thing with Jamie. She's my girlfriend."

The smug smile that crossed his face made me want to deck him. "Hear she's quite the piece of work. I'd watch out for her. She's just like her daddy."

I scowled in his direction. He didn't know Jamie. "How the fuck would you know?"

He took a step closer in my direction. "Ryan Rae was a badass sheriff, but he gave up and ran from his problems. I hear his daughter is the same way. I wouldn't bet on finding her, especially if she's running from something."

I nudged his hand from my bicep. "Jamie wouldn't run from me." *At least not anymore.*

"Maybe it's not you she's running from."

He was right. She was hiding from the person who signed their name as *Rod* in white ink. "I'm going to find whoever's hunting her, and make them wish they'd picked a different target."

The goon raised a brow, then to my surprise gave me a respectful nod. "I like your spunk."

My frown deepened. "This is way more than spunk. I'm going to find Jamie, whether you and the entire police force in Florida are going to help me or not."

He smiled at me. "Hendry is a great detective. He won't steer you wrong. He's from Point Canal. I'm sure once he talks to Rae he won't be able to put the case down until he finds her."

"I sure hope so."

"I normally go with Hendry everywhere. Let me give you my card."

I reluctantly took the small index card. "Officer Grimson?"

"That's me. He's Slaydor." He pointed his thumb behind him where the other goon was talking to the receptionist. "If you can't get a hold of Hendry, call me. I'm your next best man."

Or a kiss ass who wants to make detective. "Thanks."

"Oh, and sorry about Slaydor taking you down earlier." The amusement was clear in his voice. I turned to leave, not bothering to say goodbye.

***

The hospital was the next place I needed to visit. Tyler texted, informing me that the social worker from last night was willing to meet with us again since we'd had some time to wrap our heads around the situation. I couldn't speak for Tyler, but I was still confused as hell. Jamie being gone wasn't helping my head to clear.

I was sure Becca and Tyler would be in Nathan's room, and I wasn't in the mood for their company. Don't get me wrong, I love Becca, but I was still pissed off that she didn't know anything about Jamie's stalker and I was surprised I didn't get an earful from Tyler for being a dick to her earlier this morning.

"Hey," Tyler greeted as I walked into Nathan's room. He was sitting next to Nathan's bed, his elbows on his knees as he watched the machines. "He's still breathing."

"That's a good thing." I pulled one of the chairs to sit on the other side of Nathan's bed. "Saw the detective this morning," I grumbled. "I haven't decided if I like him or not."

Tyler's lip twitched. "There's that Conklin trust issue."

I scowled at him.

He shook his head. "We have problems with authority. Especially when it comes to control. Let me guess, he told you to back off and let him do his job?"

My scowl deepened, and he chuckled. "They want to find her just as bad as you do. Did her parents get a hold of you?"

"Yeah, ran into them at the station. I figured I'd give them the key to Jamie's condo. Hope you and Becca don't mind but I know they're short on cash."

At that moment, it occurred to me that Jamie sent her parents' money. I needed to remember to write a check and send it to their house, or something. Just because Jamie was gone didn't mean their bills would be gone. Since Jamie felt like she was a part of me, so did her family, and I wanted to take care of them, too.

Tyler shook his head. "That's fine with me. Becs and I can stay at the same hotel as Mom. She'll be here shortly." His expression turned hard when he said Becca's name. "By the way, *never* talk to my wife like that again."

I sighed deeply. "I'm sorry. I just find it hard to believe that Becca lived with Jamie for so long and never noticed these signs."

"Becca doesn't prod, and neither does Jamie. That's why they're friends. I think it's obvious Jamie didn't want anyone to know about this guy. Maybe the name will ring a bell to her parents?"

I hadn't thought of that. Their hearts would break if Hendry showed them those letters. Finding out some creep was stalking their daughter wasn't going to go well, especially with her father being a past sheriff.

"Hopefully. But what if she wasn't taken?" My heart pounded in my chest when I replayed the questions Hendry asked. "What if it was something else?"

Tyler leaned back in his seat. "Something else?"

My eyes moved to Nathan's pale, beat up face. "Do you think they were more?"

Tyler's eyes moved from me to Nathan. "Jamie and Nathan?" He laughed. "You do know he's gay, right?"

"Yes, of course, but they were obviously... close. Maybe she was different for him?"

Tyler smiled. "No. I think it's pretty clear she has eyes for you."

My neck craned in his direction. "What?"

Tyler laughed. "The sexual tension between you two is ridiculous. Jamie with Nathan doesn't give that type of vibe at all. I mean they're friends, but nothing more. You can even ask Becca."

The tightness in my chest faded when I looked at Tyler's reassuring smile. "Maybe we should get a male nurse in here. Eh, Nathan?" Tyler gently patted Nathan's thigh, and we both watched the monitors. No change happened from Tyler's comment, and the reality of Nathan being in a coma sunk in for both of us.

"He's going to be okay," I encouraged as I watched Tyler try to hide his emotion. He simply nodded, his hand patting Nathan's thigh again.

My phone buzzed in my pocket. It was Leslie. It had been nearly four hours since I was at the station. "Hello?" I answered while standing to go into the hall.

"Hi. Oh, Mitch, that was terrible," her voice was raspy from crying. "Some of the questions he asked…" She sniffled again. "I've never felt like a worse mother."

My anger for Hendry escalated. "You're an amazing mother. Don't let that asshole make you think otherwise."

"How could I have not known someone was tormenting my daughter?" Her voice was laced with anger. "Did you know? Did she tell you?"

I nearly choked on my words. "No. I just found the letters this morning. Leslie, if I had known, I would have done something. I wouldn't have left her alone."

"He asked me a lot of questions about you. I didn't know what to say. We've only known each other for so long... I'm afraid..."

Her shaky voice had my nerves on high alert. "Afraid, what?"

"I'm afraid the detective thinks the attack on Nathan is revenge toward Jamie. I'm so scared for my baby. What if this monster is hurting her?" Her voice cracked more as gasps of air broke her words. Fuck, I couldn't handle listening to this. Before I could get a word in, she continued. "He thinks Nathan and Jamie had a different relationship. Is that true? Were they a couple at some point? I mean the way she looked at you when the two of you visited for the twins' birthday, I thought for sure she'd be wearing a white dress in a year's time."

My eyes crinkled closed. Her mom saw it, too. Jamie waiting for me in a white dress would be heaven. There was no way she was into Nathan like that, not anymore. Fuck Hendry. He needed to stop making shit up to get a rise out of Jamie's family and friends. Especially her mother.

"No, Nathan and Jamie were only friends. Can I take you and Ryan out to dinner?"

"That's very kind of you, but I'm not up to eating. I just want to find my daughter."

I rubbed my eyes with my free hand. I didn't feel like eating either, but I wanted to see her parents. "I understand. Do you have a key to Jamie's place?"

She sniffled again. "No, I don't. I didn't want to bother her to give me one. She's always been so private, and I didn't want to invade her space at the time. But now I wish I would have pressed her more about what she'd been up to."

Her deep, shaky breaths revealed her guilty conscious. "This isn't your fault. I'll meet you at Jamie's house whenever you're ready. Just give me a call or a text. I'm at the hospital now."

"Oh my goodness! I didn't even ask how your brother was. Forgive me."

"You've got good reason to be sidetracked. He's stable now, but he's in a coma from lack of oxygen. We won't know more until he wakes up on his own."

"This whole situation is just terrible." She'd hit the nail on the head right there. My heart was all kinds of broken.

Before I could reply, I noticed my mother walking frantically toward me. Her long blonde hair was flowing from her speed as her heels clicked rapidly. She was always put together, but the closer she got the distress was apparent on her face. Her green eyes were wet and her lip quivered when our eyes met.

"I've got to get going. Please, let me know when you need me to let you into Jamie's place." I hung up the phone and held my arms open wide for my petite mother.

"Mitchell," she breathed, her small body pressing against mine. "Where is he?"

I unwrapped one arm from her, keeping the other around her shoulder to guide her into Nathan's room. "He's doing okay. He just looks like he's sleeping."

Her shoulders shuddered against my arm. "I don't understand how this happened."

I rubbed her bicep trying to give her comfort. Once we passed the threshold of Nathan's room, she gasped, covering her mouth with both hands. Tyler stood and paced toward our mother.

"He's okay, Mom."

She held one arm out to Tyler while reaching for my hand with the other. "I'm so happy both you boys are here." She squeezed my hand when she spoke. We were never good at being a 'family'. Only when my father died did we start trying.

Tyler nodded as he guided her to sit in the chair next to Nathan. "Of course we would be."

Tears flowed from her eyes as she set both hands on Nathan's arm and examined him. Tyler stood behind her, arms crossed and heavy in thought. Or maybe he was fighting back tears himself. My chest tightened at the sight of my family so distressed. My heart was racing, trying to figure out what direction to go into next.

"Nathan," my mother murmured in a scolding tone. "What were you up to?" She began to weep, her head falling on Nathan's forearm. She never was good at being strong. Hopefully, she wouldn't turn to the bottle, but I knew better than to think she wouldn't.

Once she lifted her head and wiped away her tears. She wanted the details. Reliving them was horrible, making me break out into a sweat and shivering while explaining how I found Nathan and did everything I could to bring him back to life.

She jumped out of her chair and pulled me to her, holding me the best she could. Before I knew it, we were in a group hug, Tyler's arms embracing us while hot tears fell down his cheeks.

"Excuse me?" The woman from last night timidly knocked on the side of the open door. The three of us parted, all wiping our eyes as though something had gotten into them. "You must be Mrs. Conklin?" She greeted. "I'm Amanda, Nathan's social worker. It's wonderful to meet you."

"Hi, please call me Mary."

She nodded and held out her hand to my mother. "I came to check on Nathan and your family. Do you have any questions?"

"I have tons," my mother sniffed.

I turned to leave. I wasn't in the mood to hear more half-ass answers from this chick. "I'm going to go check on Jamie's parents. Call me if anything changes."

***

"Where the hell are you?"

I winced as Tony, my assistant, barked into my phone. We'd just started the beginning stages of Kobiashi's amusement park that week, and he was already pissed I didn't make it on the first day.

"Sorry, I've had a really shitty past forty-eight hours."

"Yeah, I've seen the news. What the fuck is going on?"

Great, it was on the news. I should have known by Nathan's growing name. Not to mention Kobiashi owned half of Miami, and that big of an incident happening on one of his up and coming projects wouldn't go unnoticed by reporters. "Nathan's in a coma."

Silence passed over the phone. *"What?"*

"I found him barely alive."

Tony paused again. "Let's go to the bar."

Now he was talking my language. Drinking might make sharing my story easier for the umpteenth time. We agreed on a bar, and within fifteen minutes I was there with a beer in front of me. Tony was there in another twenty.

"That's some fucked up shit," he said in bewilderment after I spilled the past events. "And they don't know where Jamie is?" I shook my head while bouncing my leg. "I always thought she was a mysterious one to begin with."

I snapped my head in his direction. "What are you saying? This was her fault?"

Tony put his hands in the air. "Whoa, whoa, calm down, killer. I only meant she always seemed to be hiding something. Being stalked wasn't what I expected. A late night escort maybe." I glared at him, causing him to chuckle.

"Did you finally get her in the sack?"

My brows furrowed even more.

"You did! You have to give me details."

I punched his shoulder.

"Ouch, I was kidding. Damn, so I take it things with her weren't experimental?"

I shook my head. Nothing about Jamie was an experiment. Tony took a swig of his beer and didn't say anything more. His silence was good company but didn't help distract me from my racing mind. Only a few months ago Jamie was at this very bar, drinking a beer and laughing with me. I'd been so close to schmoozing her home with me, but she was one tough cookie. I loved that about her. She was a challenge, and I was determined to chase her to the ends of the earth. Even more so now.

My phone buzzed in my pocket, and with tired eyes, I read the screen.

Leslie Rae: The detective is about to make a public statement on channel eight news. Hopefully someone will call with information about seeing her.

A flash of hope shot through my veins as I read her text. "Hey, Tori, can you turn that TV to channel eight?"

The bleach blonde bartender with tattoos turned to me with a smile. "Sure thing." She grabbed the remote and changed the channel. I stood on my toes as if getting closer to the TV would make Hendry declare Jamie found.

Speaking of the fucker, there he stood behind a podium, his hair slicked back as it was before. He was young for a detective, and with my luck, this was probably his first case.

As of yesterday afternoon, Nathan Conklin of Conklin Architecture and Construction was attacked while visiting a construction site on Sixth and Canal. His body was found and resuscitated and is currently in critical condition at the Jackson Memorial Hospital. His co-worker, Jamie Rae, was allegedly with him at the time. Her personal belongings were left on the ground next to Mr. Conklin, but Jamie's whereabouts are currently unknown and the City of Miami has declared Jamie Rae to be a missing person. The Miami Police Department is taking all necessary actions to find Ms. Rae. Foul play has not yet been declared, and no other suspects are currently at stake. We will continue to speak with close family members of both Nathan and Jamie to help solve this case and find the attacker.

If you have any information regarding her whereabouts, please contact the phone number on the bottom of the screen.

"Foul Play?" Tony asked curiously.

My eyes squinted as I watched the television. Did Hendry think Jamie did this?

CHAPTER FOURTEEN

Jamie

Warmth.

I'm overpowered by it. My limbs are too weak to push away the heat that's covering me. A gentle rise and fall pressed against my back while the arm draped around my waist snuggled closer. Soft breaths caressed my ear, and for a moment, I felt safe and protected with the body surrounding me.

I imagined the past week with closed eyes, visions of Mitch's strong hands grasping my waist, the stubble on his chin tickling the shell of my ear as he whispered the dirty things he wanted to do to me. He must have slipped into my condo last night, the naughty man he was. I wiggled my backside into him, groaning slightly so he knew I was happy he'd surprised me with his presence in bed.

His arm clung to me tighter while his hips moved forward to greet my behind, his cheek now nuzzling into my neck. The gesture was affectionate, and something I'd never let any other man do. He'd mended the scars that developed from the torture I had received earlier in my life. The way he'd gently kiss along my nape, healing me with his unconditional love was the best remedy I could have ever asked for.

No stubble scraped against my neck as his lips pressed against my jaw. It was strange for his face to feel so smooth, especially in the morning. His facial hair grew fast, normally prickly by the evening. No matter, he turned me on whether he had stubble or not. And now that he was in my bed, I was ready to go, wanting his erection poking against my lower back to fill me completely.

I reached for his hand, guiding it underneath my T-shirt to cup one heavy breast.

"Mmm," I groaned under my breath as his thumb and pointer finger pinched my nipple. His mouth opened against my skin, hot air causing goose bumps to form, making my core ache for him.

The T-shirt and panties felt like a parka as his mouth ravished my neck to my shoulder, then back to the outside of my earlobe. Tingles shot through me, making my toes curl and my hips squirm with want.

But his hand felt different. It was softer, not calloused from working on-site all day. My breath slowed as a dull ache formed in my head.

The smooth hand moved from my breasts down my stomach and between my now opened legs. "Greedy as ever."

That voice.

My body stiffened.

"So wet for me, even after all our time apart."

No, it couldn't be...

My eyes sprung open. The dull ache in my head was now a full on pounding, the blood pumping like sirens in my ears. I shot up, my arms crossing over my chest in the process. With a quivering lip, I turned to see the face I'd been hiding from for the past seven years.

"How...?" I gasped, the air in my lungs evaporating from fear. This wasn't my room. The king size bed with black sheets stood stark against the white walls and modern art framing them.

Rod sat up, his dirty blond hair disheveled. "Sit down before you get sick."

My chest heaved as I stared at him and my surroundings.

What happened? How did I get here? How the hell did he find me? Where the hell am I?

The room began to spin as I sucked in deep breaths for air, my body lurching over as I found my knees. I coughed as I struggled to breathe, terror filling me to its max.

Rod's hand reached for my chin, lifting it so my brown eyes were on the dull blue hue of his. He licked his lips as he studied my erratic state of mind. "Calm down. You're safe. I'll answer every question you have, but you need to breathe, Jamie."

My body cringed from his touch, my eyes wide with terror. I wanted to shove him and run like hell, but I was frozen stiff, too afraid to move from the blue daggers of his eyes pinning me in place. I swallowed the large lump that formed in my throat, unsure what to do next, knowing how easy it was for him to flip. That moment where he went from being a normal, passionate guy to a psychotic monster.

Rod released my chin and stood. "Are you hungry? You've been asleep for a while."

My wobbly legs rose from the ground, my arms hugging my body. I felt so exposed in only underwear and a T-shirt.

He vanished down a small hallway, then returned with a robe, holding it for me to take at arms length. "Here." His head dipped low while his eyes found the ground. If I didn't know any better, I'd say his expression was one of embarrassment. He'd just felt me up with intentions of more, now he was acting like a shy school boy? All the more reason for me to believe he was still a lunatic.

With a tentative hand, I reached for the thigh length robe, wrapping the silky fabric tightly around my body. Moving from my spot felt impossible with Rod standing only a few feet away from me.

He sensed my apprehension. "I promise. I'm not going to hurt you. Come, you need to eat. If you don't, the…"

I cocked my head in question, waiting for him to finish his sentence. Sighing, he stepped to me, holding his hand out for me to take.

"Please."

Every inch of my skin crawled, telling me he had ulterior motives for bringing me to this place. But I had no idea what was happening, and he did say he'd answer any questions I had. I unhooked my arms from around my waist, taking his hand.

His shoulders relaxed and his lip quirked in relief, his thumb skating over my knuckles.

We walked out of the room, my eyes taking in the surroundings with each step. The ceilings were tall and angled, white walls decorated with modern art as we passed through a living area with a grand piano and fireplace. The windows were covered by blinds and drapes, hiding if it were light or dark outside.

"What time is it?" I asked with a dry throat.

"Just after four in the morning." He led me to the kitchen, pulling me to a barstool at an island facing cupboards and counters loaded with every kitchen gadget you could imagine. "Sit down, I'll make us something to eat."

The kitchen was chilly, causing me to rub my biceps for warmth. Rod noticed. "I can adjust the air conditioning if you're cold."

I nodded, watching him poke his finger on a touch screen hanging down from a cupboard. He offered me a smile, then moved to the refrigerator. "Want some eggs?"

"Okay." I furrowed my eyebrows, trying to get a grasp on what was going on. My thumbs found my temples, gently massaging the dull ache. "How did I get here?"

"I brought you," he replied nonchalantly, pulling ingredients from the fridge, then reaching above the stove for a frying pan.

"Why don't I remember?"

"You hit your head." I watched as he opened up an egg container and began cracking them into a mixing bowl. "The bump has gone down some, but you might want to ice it some more."

I closed my eyes, trying hard to think what the last memory was that I had. "How'd I hit my head?"

He moved his eyes from the eggs to glance at me for a moment, then continued his task. "You fell."

I sat there dumbfounded, my thumbs pressing into my head harder than searching for the bump. He was right, the side of my head had a nasty lump. I'd never felt more confused. Biting my lip felt like it might give me more insight, but nothing was coming. I needed to know the truth.

"So I *fell* and you just happened to come to my rescue?" Sighing, he stopped whisking and gave his full attention to me. "I don't buy it, Rod, not for a second."

His eyes fluttered closed as his shoulders relaxed. "Do you know how good it feels to hear my name come from those beautiful lips of yours?"

I gulped, fighting the head to toe tremor that pulsed through me. I wanted to tell him I hated him and all he'd put me through. His lies and deceitfulness, what he did to Landon... All of the torment I'd suffered because of *him*. I hadn't had a functional relationship in seven years because of—

Relationship.

Mitch.

Nathan.

Oh my God. *Nathan.*

It was all flooding back to me, every small detail I couldn't think of when I'd first awoke in the monster's arms. Going to breakfast and telling Nathan about my budding relationship with Mitch flashed in my mind. I clenched my hand to my stomach. I had also informed Nathan about the positive pregnancy test I'd taken that morning.

I flew to my feet, taking a few steps back, wrapping the silk nightgown tightly around my body. My voice was low and direct as I spoke. "What did you do?"

Rod's demeanor changed from soft to apprehensive, both his arms went in the air as he stepped around the island toward me. "Just calm down."

"What did you do?" I shouted, demanding answers. "Where's Nathan?"

His eyes got dark when I said Nathan's name, and that same pathetic fear took over, causing me to step backward into the living area and against a sofa table. Rod's strides were long and lean as he approached me, the piercing look he gave me, causing my breath to come to a complete halt.

His jaw was clenched as he spoke. "I really want you to eat before we start talking about what happened."

We were face to face now, Rod's stature dominating mine. He let out a heavy breath from his nose as he closed his eyes. When they opened again, the anger had simmered, and longing filled them. One hand brushed the hair from the side of my face, caressing my cheek. I stiffened as his fingers trailed my skin, worried he'd strangle me if I didn't comply with his demands.

"Let me take care of you first, then I'll explain," he whispered, his lips mere inches from mine. He wanted to kiss me, it was obvious by the pleading look in his eyes, but I wanted nothing to do with his touch.

Even though I was sickened by his presence, I nodded and walked past him to the kitchen island, knowing that's what he'd need if I were to ever get any answers.

"We can talk while I cook." It was as though it was my reward for settling down. Finding his way back to the ingredients he'd pulled out earlier, he took out a large knife from a drawer and began chopping vegetables.

"Okay. Let's start with, where are we?"

"This was one of my grandfather's homes. He gave it to me a few years ago."

"Are we still in Florida?"

He was quiet as though he didn't want me to know where exactly he'd taken me.

"Yes."

"Miami?"

"Does it matter?"

"I wouldn't have asked if I didn't find it important."

He threw the veggies he was chopping into the pan along with some olive oil, gently mixing them around. "No, we're not in Miami. We're about an hour north from there." I frowned, knowing that was the most direct answer about the location he was willing to give.

He laid his palms flat on the counter. "You have to know something. I've gotten help. I realize how I treated you before was inexcusable behavior." I raised a brow.

"I never should have been so forceful and lost my temper with you. A therapist has helped me realize all of this. I've been taking medication for a few years now."

You'd think the therapist would have informed him that stalking was illegal. "Why did you send me those letters?"

A scowl formed on his brow as his eyes found the counter. "I didn't think you'd talk to me if I showed up on your doorstep."

"But a creepy letter would be better? Did your therapist know about those?" The sarcasm was clear in my voice, causing him to scowl even more.

"I knew you weren't ready to settle down yet. I wanted you to know I still cared about you. That I was waiting for you to be ready to be with me."

I was speechless. His words sounded like a normal wounded ex-boyfriend who was still madly in love with a woman, but his actions were extreme and incredibly fucked up. "How did you find me," I whispered, trying my hardest to not let my irritability show. "Every time I went somewhere new, you always found me. How?"

He moved back to the stove while I spoke, fussing with the egg mixture so it wouldn't burn. "I didn't always know where you were." His words were pained. "It was a pretty low point in my life." He turned to me, a spark flashing in his eyes. "Then I found you again. It was as if the universe was handing you to me. There you were, getting out of a white Lexus at Acqualia."

My eyes widened. Acqualia was where I'd been living while in Miami.

"I'd been working there as a security guard. I know, not ideal, but like I said I was at a low point in my life."

"So you don't run the police anymore?"

Rod's lip quirked. "Not exactly."

"Do you work at all?"

"Yes," he clipped, obviously wanting the conversation to go in a different direction. "I wanted to approach you so many times, but didn't know how."

"So you thought the letters would work?"

He shrugged, removing the egg mixture from the stove and distributing it to two different plates. "You seemed so happy and full of life. I was falling in love with you all over again."

My stomach sank. I looked happy because I had started a new life without him. My job was kick ass and my friends were amazing. No part of that happiness was created from him. I couldn't meet his eyes when he sat next to me, placing the food and a fork in front of me. If I ate anything, I'd end up hurling.

"I started taking my therapist more seriously. Following the steps he'd talked about. I was finally ready to knock on your door and beg for you to give me another chance. I even brought flowers. But I saw you with *someone*." His eyes closed tight as his fists formed balls, the white of his knuckles showing. He didn't say anything as his jaw ticked. After around ten seconds, they opened again, and his hands flexed, causing the blood to flow back into his fingers. One arm slid on the back of my stool, his eyes intense as they studied me.

"I tried to make excuses for you and that guy. But I'd seen you with other men before *him*. You never looked at those meatheads the same way. You looked at *him* how you used to look at me. I should have known. This guy was intelligent, rich, and held your attention."

My eyes found my lap as my hands protectively wrapped around my stomach. Now I knew why Mitch got so jealous when I was around Nathan. We did have a special connection, there was no denying that.

Rod moved the curtain of hair that was hiding my face, his hand lingering on the shell of my ear. "I couldn't lose you again."

I shook my head, standing. "Where's Nathan?"

Rod stood with me. "You don't need to worry about him anymore."

"He's my friend," I said through clenched teeth, my eyes fighting the threat of tears. His head fell to the side, the look of shame slightly passing over his face.

I shook my head rapidly. "You killed him, didn't you? Is that your answer for everything? Murdering anyone who gets in the way? I bet your therapist would be proud!" Tears sprung from my eyes now as I spun away from him. "Where are my things? My phone? I want to go home."

"Stop. You're not going anywhere," he demanded, catching my arm before I could get away.

"What's going to stop me?" I shouted, trying to yank my arm away.

"I've got resources. Don't make me use them," he threatened. "I won't hurt you, but that doesn't mean everyone else will stay safe."

I screamed at him in frustration, knowing he spoke the truth. "You already killed Landon and Nathan. Who else are you going to take from me?"

"I didn't kill your brother, and you know that."

More tears fell down my cheeks as the guilt I constantly lived with turned the knife in my heart. Damn Rod and his good for nothing grandfather. They tampered with evidence and twisted my brother's death, hurting more people that I loved in the process, including killing my brother's best friend.

"I didn't kill Nathan, either." My eyes narrowed at him skeptically. "It's all over the news." He pulled me against my will into the living room, forcing me to sit on the couch as he reached for the remote. "You can see for yourself."

I stopped fighting him, and after a moment he let go of my arm, then turned the television on, flipping to the news channel. Sure enough, there he was in his expensively tailored suit. The picture on the screen was a still from the photo shoot he took with Tyler for Forbes magazine. Rod sat next to me, intently watching my reaction to the screen. He shut it off before the news anchor could finish talking but I'd heard enough. My body was shivering on the inside, knowing the puzzle pieces to Rod's sick game were all falling into place. I was missing and suspicious, most likely looking like I was running from committing a crime.

"T-That's not true," I stuttered. "I didn't hurt him. I was trying to save him."

"No, you didn't. But police don't know who attacked him either."

Shaking my head, I asked quietly. "So what happens now?"

His arm skated across my thighs and to my hip. "We start our life together."

My eyes squeezed shut, fighting every urge inside that told me to scream and throw a fit. But I knew better. Rod's games weren't ones to be tampered with. "What about my family?"

His thumb caressed my hip. "They'll stay safe if you cooperate." A lone tear rolled down my cheek, and Rod caught it with his lips, my skin burning in the process. "I just want another shot, Jamie. Think about how you felt when we were first together, how we were inseparable. The second that deputy took his lunch you were on my lap."

His hand crept from my hip to my knee, pulling my legs so they were over his thighs, forcing my body to turn in his direction. It felt disgusting to be so close to him. "I'm going to remind you how good we were together, how much love we had. Show you I can be the man of your dreams again."

A million tiny prickles formed on my skin as his hands found my cheeks. The real man of my dreams was probably doubting everything I'd said to him. Maybe if I'd told Mitch I loved him he would have faith in me, and would cross the ocean to find me, but right now, I had no idea if his heart was still mine. I was trapped with a dangerous man who was obsessed with me, and would go to extremes to make me his.

But Rod never said anything about Mitch. He thought I was in love with Nathan. And if he thought I was in love with Nathan then maybe Mitch would be safe.

"I want a life with you. I can give you anything you've ever wanted."

"Anything?" I asked quietly, trying to mentally give myself a pep talk to go through with what I was about to do to find my happy ending. The new life that was growing inside of me needed to be protected, and it was my job to keep the little piece of Mitch that I had left safe.

"The world is yours, my love. Money isn't an issue. I have more than enough. Your family will stay safe. We'll see them again when I think you're ready. When they'll be accepting of us." His breath was hot on my cheek, the moistness of his lips settling on my skin, making me want to vomit.

"It's hard to remember, especially when it's been so long," I murmured, my hands still trembling around my waist.

"I think I can refresh your memory. You just need to open your mind and let me in again."

My eyes fluttered open to meet his gaze. Those baby blues had hypnotized me in the past, but then I remembered they belonged to the demon that haunted my nightmares.

"I'm going to kiss you." His voice deepened as he leaned closer.

How the hell am I going to do this? The thought of Rod's lips touching me made me want to jump into an incinerator, but I had to play the part. I needed to do this if I was ever going to see Mitch again. Rod had to think the baby growing inside of me was his, because who knew what he would do if he found out I was pregnant with someone else's baby.

Our noses touched first while his hands slinked from my cheeks down my shoulders and biceps. "You're trembling. Please, don't be afraid. You're the most precious person to me. I won't hurt you."

Swallowing the huge lump in my throat, I tilted forward, giving him permission to plant his lips on mine. A groan of relief slipped through his lips with his gentle pluck, his own hands quivering as they wrapped around my waist, pulling me to his chest. I couldn't move my arms from my stomach, needing to keep them there to help get me through this. To protect what mattered most.

His passion turned more dominant, his hands running along my spine and to the back of my head, pulling me in deeper as his lips begged for me to open to him. I reluctantly obeyed, cautiously opening my mouth and letting his tongue touch mine.

My gut was flipping, my chest feeling like a stake was shoved dead through the center of my heart for letting this man touch me so intimately. He pried my shaking hands from my stomach, pulling them so they wrapped around his neck as he kissed me. He wanted the connection so badly, I could feel his need radiating from his skin through each mangled breath.

Rod moved my body slowly, guiding me flat on the couch while he hovered over top of me, our lips never parting in the process. My chest tightened, knowing he'd soon overpower me. My hands clamped down on his T-shirt, grasping the fabric in attempts to keep myself calm.

Only Mitch was allowed to let his body press against mine so dominantly. He was the one allowed to take control, leading me to a love stricken high. But Mitch wasn't here. He wasn't kissing me with unobtainable passion.

Rod reluctantly pulled his mouth from mine, allowing me to take a deep, shaky breath. He stood from the couch unexpectedly, but only to pull me with him, burying his hands in my hair to kiss me again. I could feel his erection pressing harder into my stomach with each deep thrust of his tongue into my mouth, and it took everything in me not to gag.

"Feel this?" His voice was husky as he began walking backward, pulling me along with him. "Those sparks? The connection?" I nodded, my swollen eyes never meeting his as we moved down the hall. "Don't fight the feelings I'm going to revive in you."

We were in his room again, the bed with disheveled sheets hitting the backs of Rod's knees as we came to a halt. The guilt and betrayal consumed me with what I was about to let happen. "I want to touch every inch of you," Rod murmured against my ear as his hands roamed down my waist and to my thighs. "Please, don't be scared."

His hands left me to remove his T-shirt, revealing the strong definition on his chest and torso. But nothing compared to Mitch. Rod was smaller, his shoulders not as broad and his biceps not as big.

You have to do this to keep Mitch safe. To save what we created together.

I leaned my head against his chest, my clammy hands resting on his lower back just above his boxers. To Rod, it passed as an affectionate hug, but really I needed the moment to gain more courage. *You have to do this.*

Rod sat down on the bed, pulling me to stand between his legs. I moved my hands to his shoulders, my thumbs methodically moving on the back of his neck. "Let me feel you," he whispered, his hands finding the belt of the robe and untying it. His pace was agonizingly slow as he removed the silky fabric and tossed it to the floor.

He has to believe I'm going to give him a shot.

I have to do this to keep everyone I love safe.

Rod gently removed my T-shirt, his eyes turning hungry as he took me in from head to toe. He licked his lips as his hands glided under my panties, pulling them down to my ankles. Tears burned my eyes as I looked away from him, biting my lip to keep it from trembling. I couldn't keep the terrified shivers from taking over my body as his fingers roamed. Now was the time to turn all of my emotions off, and find that dark hole in my head where I could curl up and be numb.

"Help me remember how it used to be," I spoke in barely a whisper.

The moment Rod's body finally went limp on top of me, a heavy breath shuddered from my lips. He gently rolled to the side, his arm wrapping around my waist as he snuggled next to me. I rolled in the opposite direction. I couldn't face him.

Rod moved to spoon me, his hand gently gliding across the curve of my hip to my thigh. "I'm sorry." His nose pressed against the back of my neck. "I wasn't planning on getting physical so quickly. I wanted to gain your trust back, make sure you were comfortable."

Containing my sniffles was impossible. Rod pulled me closer, his mouth finding my ear. "It's okay if you thought of him just now. I understand it's going to take time for you to find our love again." A shudder pulsed through my body. His hand wrapped around me, finding mine and squeezing it. "I promise I'll make all your dreams come true."

You just destroyed them. "I believe you," I lied.

He stayed cuddled around me for what felt like forever. Eventually, he stood. I tried to fake sleeping, but he knew better. With my eyes closed, I could feel him returning and sitting down next to me. "Until I can trust you, I'm going to have to do this, baby."

A poke to my neck caused me to twitch, but after a few breaths, I was floating.

CHAPTER FIFTEEN

Mitch

Flames might as well have burst out of my head as I marched into Hendry's office the following morning. After his statement, news reporters were twisting the story, saying Jamie looked guilty. Probably because that fucker mentioned the words *foul play*.

"Where the fuck is Hendry?" I demanded, not bothering to wait in line behind the other citizens.

The woman stood, pinning me with her eyes. "Mr. Conklin, I suggest you wait in line like everyone else. Otherwise, your ass is going to be knocked down again."

The big thug stood behind her, throwing his paper on the seat he'd been sitting on. "You sure have trouble listening."

"I have trouble with cops who don't do anything," I hissed.

His eyes darkened as he moved from behind the glass to the front lobby, grabbing my shirt and throwing me against the wall. "Say that again, I dare you."

His eyes were cold as they glared into mine. I didn't care, I gave it right back to him, shoving him off of me. "Do your fucking job and go find Hendry."

Grimson came out of nowhere. "Leave him be, Slaydor. Come on, Mr. Conklin."

Nudging myself free from Slaydor, I gave him the best glare I could. If he weren't in a uniform, he'd be flat on his ass by my fist.

Grimson walked through a door, talking into his walkie as we moved. "Hendry. Mitch Conklin is here as you suspected."

I scowled. How the hell did he know I'd be here?

This time, I was brought to an actual office. I was surprised when I saw Jamie's parents sitting across from Hendry. Leslie was weeping on Ryan's shoulder. Ryan looked apprehensive.

"Glad my intuition isn't wrong regarding you, Conklin. Grimson, can you get him a chair? I called Jamie's parents in this morning because the security camera in the retail store across from Plaza Towers captured something very interesting."

My eyes widened. Did they see Nathan's attacker? Maybe they saw who took Jamie? Grimson placed a chair next to Ryan, but I was too anxious to sit. "Can I see it?"

Hendry looked to Leslie and Ryan for permission, while Grimson stood off to the side. Ryan nodded to Hendry, his arm wrapping tightly around Leslie.

"First, I'll play Jamie's 911 call. This happened at 10:52am."

The muffle of the 911 operator's voice was loud and clear, then there was Jamie's distraught voice. It tore at my heart to hear her stumble over her words. I could hear the stress and fear in her voice.

Yes, I need an ambulance at the Tower Plaza. I have a thirty-two-year-old male with a bad wound. It's bleeding, a lot."

"I'll send someone right away. What happened to him?" the operator asked.

"I'm not sure. It won't stop bleeding!"

Then there was a faint voice in the background that sounded an awful lot like Nathan's did when he was fighting for his life.

"Jamie... go... I'll be..."

Static crackled, then Jamie's voice was farther away. *"Nathan, please."*

The operator was asking questions, but the voices rang clear in the background.

"You're going to be fine. I love you." My eyes closed in pain. How she said I love you felt so personal, so emotional.

"Jay... no..."

Her last words were loud and clear.

"I'm so sorry."

The line went dead, and my heart pounded faster.

Both Hendry and Grimson watched me carefully as I processed what I'd just heard. Hendry cleared his throat and turned his computer, making the screen face us. "Now, this footage was captured approximately ten minutes after the 911 call was made."

My eyes watched in horror at the screen, waiting to see what asshole would be dragging Jamie out kicking and screaming.

But it wasn't a man. My heart was crushed when I saw the fuzzy picture on the screen. It was a woman, dressed in skinny jeans and a fitted T-shirt, walking across the street to a white Lexus. Her long caramel hair whispered in the wind, and her stride was quick as can be as she hopped into the front seat. Her face wasn't shown, but the way her slender hips swayed looked a lot like Jamie's. I sank into the chair Grimson brought, my hands covering my mouth as my eyes were glued to the screen. Leslie let out a low heave as Hendry replayed the short video.

"It can't be," I croaked, my hand still covering my mouth. "Jamie wouldn't..."

"Of course she wouldn't!" Leslie yelled through sobs. "Jamie would never hurt anyone!"

Hendry offered a sympathetic glance. "We never want to believe the worst in our children, Mrs. Rae. But she looks an awful lot like Jamie, and she's getting into a car that matches her license plate."

Ryan stood, his chair forcefully sliding backward. "I don't believe it! It's too fuzzy, there's no way that's her!"

"Why would she apologize to Nathan?" Hendry asked Ryan. "Why would she say an 'I love you' that seemed like a final goodbye?"

I stood next to Ryan. "Maybe because she knew he was dying and some murderer was about to stab her too, and she knew she had to get out of there."

Hendry sighed heavily through his nose. "We need to find Jamie, and unfortunately, this footage doesn't help."

"I know she sounded," I sighed, hating the words about to come out of my mouth. "...intimate. But Nathan and Jamie weren't like that." Now would be the time to out my brother, but I couldn't do it. He didn't need to wake up to any more revealing secrets on the news, especially some so personal. I shook my head. "Besides, Jamie wouldn't wear jeans to meet with our biggest client."

Ryan looked hopeful in my direction. "Mitch is right. Jamie rarely wears jeans as it is."

Hendry scratched his head. "I'll try to track her car. I've already radioed her license plate to the State of Florida police."

Ryan nodded, but that answer wasn't good enough for me. He was accusing Jamie of trying to kill Nathan. My anger wasn't going to be contained for much longer. "Why would she try to kill Nathan? It makes no sense. They were best friends!" My hand slammed on the desk. Grimson put his hand on my shoulder, forcing me to sit back down.

"I'm meeting with people from your business. Maybe I'll find out more information. Did Nathan leave anything to Jamie?"

My head shook drastically. "You think this is about money? Why the hell would she run if that were the scenario? Your angles are way off."

Hendry stood, his eyes becoming stormy. "I have to look at every angle possible, Mr. Conklin. That's my job."

I bit my tongue, wanting to curse at him and tell him how much of an idiot I thought he was. Ryan's hand found my shoulder, his attempt to calm me down. He obviously knew how to react in these types of situations, and he also knew the wrong way to act. "We'll figure this out," he said evenly, his hand pushing me to sit back down in my seat. I obeyed his firm grasp.

"How long will it take you to get the footage from the other stores and gas stations?"

"I should receive the rest of them this afternoon, and I plan on reviewing them overnight and into tomorrow."

Ryan nodded. My eyes passed between the two of them, trying to read the vibe Ryan was getting from Hendry. He seemed to agree with Hendry's process, but I still thought he could be doing more.

Hendry's voice calmed with Ryan's patient response. "Why don't the three of you go search Miami? Maybe think about friends that are out of town where Jamie could flee."

"She's not fleeing!" Leslie wept, her hands pounding against Hendry's desk. "I know my daughter, and that wasn't her. I don't care what any of you say." She stood from her seat, forcefully moving her chair as she left the room. Ryan sighed, giving Hendry an apologetic lift of an eyebrow.

"Come on, Mitch," Ryan urged as he stood from his chair. "Leslie needs to get back to Jamie's to process all of this.

Leslie reached for Ryan's arm. "I'm sorry, Detective, I don't mean to be upset with you."

Hendry offered her a sincere smile that was filled with pity. "I understand. This is close to home for me too, Mr. and Mrs. Rae. Point Canal was where I got my feet on the ground."

Ryan shook Hendry's hand. "That you did. Thanks again. Keep us posted."

Hendry nodded with a kind smile to Ryan and Leslie, but his expression turned into a frown when he watched me walk by him.

***

"Tell me you don't think the girl in the surveillance was Jamie," I whispered once Ryan closed the door to Jamie's bedroom where Leslie had fallen asleep.

Ryan ran a hand through his short hair. "I don't want to think it's her." We both sat on the couch. "There's no way they can identify her on such a fuzzy video, but Hendry's working with what he's got."

I huffed, leaning my head back until it thudded against the wall. "I don't like him."

Ryan mimicked me, his head touching the wall as well. "Most people don't like good detectives. He was young when he was in Point Canal with me, but it was only for a short time. I didn't know him that well, but I remember the ones who couldn't cut it as a cop, and Hendry held his own. The case is in good hands, Mitch. You need to trust the officers to do their job."

I closed my eyes, not wanting to hear what Ryan was telling me.

"Let's go for a drive. Maybe we'll find something," Ryan said, patting my knee and standing from the couch.

"I'll drive," I said with determination. Even though Ryan had faith in Hendry, I still didn't believe in the egotistical asshole.

CHAPTER SIXTEEN

Jamie

It was dark when my groggy body finally awakened. There was movement in the room, but I couldn't focus enough to know what was going on. My hands rubbed my face. The asshole had drugged me. Gaining his trust so I could escape this fortress was going to be difficult.

Just as I was starting to sit up, Rod entered, holding a mug. "Feeling okay? I brought you some juice." He sat next to me, offering me the drink.

"What time is it?"

He glanced at his watch. "About 7:30 p.m. You've been sleeping for a while. Probably from your head injury."

"Or whatever drug you injected into me," I mumbled, taking the drink from him and examining it.

His lip quirked. "Such a smart little cookie, you are. Don't worry, nothing's in that drink."

I rolled my eyes as I drank it. Rod smiled. "I'll make you dinner, but first, I'm going to take a shower."

He was going to take a shower? *Leaving me out in the open and able to leave?* My heart started to race, my body screaming at me to calm down. Rod moved to kiss my forehead, then left to the back of the bedroom. I heard the shower and swung my legs from under the sheets and onto the floor.

That's when I noticed the heavy band wrapped around my ankle. *That fucker.* He'd put a tracking device on me. My hands flew to my ankle, tugging at the thick band. There was no way I'd be able to remove it. The binding was too strong, and looked to require a passcode.

Screw this.

I jumped from the bed, grabbing the T-shirt I'd reluctantly taken off earlier this morning and threw it on, not bothering to look for the panties that Rod tossed this morning as well.

I moved quickly through the tall ceilinged house, making my way to the extravagant kitchen. Searching the drawers for a knife.

The drawers slammed as I opened and closed them, until I reached one that wouldn't budge. I yanked with all my might, suppressing a grunt of frustration in the process, moving to the cabinets. Damn, they were locked too! My hands found my head as I leaned into the cupboard. Of course he'd lock drawers with sharp objects. He probably figured I'd try and slit his throat.

"What are you looking for?"

That was a quick shower. I took a deep breath, swallowing to steady my voice. "I thought I'd make dinner for you." The sweetness I was going for didn't come through in my scratchy voice as I moved to the fridge.

Rod chuckled under his breath as he moved toward me, leaning back on the sink with his hands grasping the edge of the counter. At a slight glance, I noticed his shirt was off and his jersey shorts were low on his hips. "You sure that was your original intention when coming in the kitchen?"

My jaw clenched. I wanted to fight with him, but I knew that's what he was fishing for. "Kitchen's are used for cooking, and I haven't eaten real food in a while." I forced a flirt. "Since someone wouldn't let me eat this morning."

He laughed softly, pushing off the counter and coming behind me while I rummaged through the fridge. "I told you we didn't have to," he whispered, his hands finding my thighs, then running underneath my T-shirt and to my bare hips.

I choked back emotion while his hands wandered. "If you don't want me to touch you like this, just say the word and I'll stop."

My heart hissed for him to back the fuck off, but my mind fought the urge to rip his fingers from my hips. "I'm a big girl. I know what I want."

His smooth hands ran across my stomach, pulling me so that my back was touching his chest. His lips found my ear. "Yes, and I know how intelligent you are. I'm sure you notice that beautiful ankle bracelet, too. I know where you are, all of the time. I know if you're in the bathroom, I know when you're lying in bed, and I know when you're trying to open doors and windows." He slowly spun me so I was facing him. His blue eyes were icy as they stared into mine. "I have eyes everywhere. Don't forget that."

With our eyes locked, he moved one hand to a drawer next to the fridge, placing his thumb against a pad. It popped open, pressing into my back. "Half of these drawers only open to my fingerprints, same with the outside doors and windows, so don't get any ideas."

My eyes closed, the feeling of being trapped sinking in deeper than it had the night before. Rod gripped my jaw with his other hand, forcing my eyes to open and look back into his. "You are mine now. Do you understand?"

My teeth clamped down on my cheeks as I slowly nodded, Rod's grip still tight on my jaw. He nodded in approval. "Let me show you around the house. Then you can shower while I start dinner."

I quietly followed him as he took my hand and led me out of the kitchen. "You've seen most of the house already. Down this hall is a spare bedroom. I intended for it to be your room, but since last night went so well..."

I inwardly melted with shame. I hated that I'd slept with him, but knew I needed to in order to escape his grasp at some point. I squeezed his hand and offered him a shy smile. He smirked in return and squeezed back.

We stopped at a door. Rod let go of my hand and swiped a few places, then pressed his palm flat on the touch screen. A buzz sounded and the door unlocked. My hope faded even more, knowing this was how all the doors were. "Upstairs is my office. A lot goes on up here. Employees are usually up here as well."

I tugged my shirt down further. He smiled. "Don't worry, no one is up there now." I nodded, a small surge of hope filling me, thinking maybe one of them would realize he had a woman being held captive.

He took my hand and began walking up the stairs. "I'd never let anyone see you dressed in only my white T-shirt."

Well, what a relief.

"And just so you know, none of my workers speak English. They live on our property as well."

God, he'd said *our*. "What language do they speak?"

His lip curved as he glanced back at me. "A rare one based in a small country from South America. You probably haven't heard of it."

I frowned as we reached the top of the stairs and into a wide space where couches and a few televisions were placed. It looked like a dorm community room. Even a foosball table was off in a corner. My stomach churned when I saw the stripper poles throughout the space.

"What type of business is this?" I gulped, suddenly feeling thankful that Rod was so possessive of me.

He followed my wide eyes as they looked at the poles. "Not what you think. Come this way, and you'll see."

He tugged my hand, leading me down another hallway with closed doors, doors I wasn't sure I wanted to open. We reached the end of the hall where another door with handprint access was needed.

"This is the greenhouse," he said proudly as his hand was being scanned.

My arms were crossed as the door slowly opened, revealing rows and rows of plants. I walked over the threshold, Rod following behind me. I didn't recognize the plants, but then again, I didn't know much. Besides, I had a feeling what Rod had going on was much bigger than selling pot to stupid experimental kids.

"What are they?"

Rod grabbed a labeled water bottle from a cart, walking over to one of the plants and spritzing it lightly. "This one is a coca plant."

My voice was a soft whisper. "You make and sell cocaine?"

His eyes flickered, matching his smile. "Correct."

The muggy, humid air felt thick as I tried to breathe. I should have known he'd be doing something illegal. He knew how the law worked, so he knew how to not get caught. And he probably still had eyes everywhere.

I rubbed my eyes, needing to wrap my head around the situation. Rod set down the water bottle and moved to me, his hands resting on my waist. "You don't need to know anything else. I just wanted you to know I earn my money. I don't steal it."

"This is wrong on so many levels," I croaked.

One of his hands brushed my hair behind my ear. "Why? Because I make a living off of people who make poor decisions? Most businesses work that way. Mine just has a bigger price tag. I live like a king, and you are my queen."

I swatted his hand away. "Your coke queen? I'm so honored."

He shook his head. "Don't be like that. I could have kept this to myself. I want you to know what I'm doing."

My arms crossed protectively over my stomach. "Is that what you stuck into my neck earlier?"

"No," he said in disgust. "I don't use that shit anymore, and neither will you." Rod licked his lips. "I wanted you to grow accustomed to this new lifestyle, I figured you'd need to have something in your system so you wouldn't worry yourself sick until you could process everything. Come on, let me show you my personal office."

I sighed, then followed him back through the heavy metal doors. We passed the closed doors again and I was glad Rod didn't show me inside. I didn't need to know.

"What's this room for? Getting your clients hooked?" I grumbled as we passed through the hang out area with stripper poles again.

Rod nodded, ignoring my snark and leading me down the stairs and past the big metal door. We walked through a roundabout hall with a few more doors with screen pads, then finally to what I assumed was his office. He took my hand and held it to the screen. "You can get into this room whenever I program for it to be okay. I want you to come see me while I'm working, just like any other couple."

The door clicked open, and I walked inside with him. It looked like a normal owner of an empire's office, except the back wall was covered with television screens. Every angle, nook, and crevice was being recorded. There was also screens of my own condo, where my mother was lying on my bed crying.

"Mom," I whispered, a tear dripping down my cheek. "She's worried about me." This was how he knew all about me. How he saw Nathan lying under the covers in my bed. How did he get a camera in my bedroom? "Please, she needs to know I'm okay."

His eyes crinkled in thought while he crossed his arms. "Not yet. She'll know soon enough."

A sob escaped my mouth. "If you hurt them, you hurt me."

His scowl deepened as he looked at his feet. I slowly took a step toward him, my hand tentatively reaching to touch his arm. "Please. I'll do anything you say, just don't hurt them any more than I already have."

Rod sighed, then his eyes met my pleading tears. "I'll give them something." His hands found my face, his forehead leaning down to touch with mine. "I need to trust you, too."

I buried my face into his chest, tears flowing freely. I didn't want him to wrap his arms around me for comfort. I wanted my mom, not him, and he was withholding her from me along with everyone else.

But I had to play the part.

I sniffed, wiping my tears from my eyes as I backed away from him. One hand found my stomach, and I rubbed it protectively. Rod noticed.

"You have to be hungry. Come on." He placed his hand on my lower back, urging me out of his office.

We walked back through the kitchen and living area, and into the bedroom. He turned left down a short hall where I assumed the bathroom was. "This is your closet. Wear whatever you like. If there's something you need, tell me, and it's yours."

The light flicked on, and I nearly gasped at the amount of clothing and shoes. Heels of all sorts, dresses, sweats, lingerie. It would be any girls dream, but it only added to my nightmare.

He watched as I circled around the room, my fingers grazing against the expensive fabrics.

"My closet is over here." He pointed his thumb over his shoulder in the opposite direction. "The master bathroom is this way." He grabbed my hand, pulling me from the closet and past another archway with taller ceilings. The bathroom was covered in beautiful tiles, and an oval bathtub was in the center, dividing the room where separate sinks and counters were.

My stomach was in knots. Rod's sick head really thought we'd live here together forever. And *peacefully?*

"Here's your side. All your cosmetics are in these cabinets. If I missed something, please tell me. The shower's hidden over this way."

I followed him, into the deep cave of a shower. A dim light flicked on by our presence. Rod slid around me, reaching to turn on the shower, the steam quickly filling the space. His hands grabbed the hem of my T-shirt, lifting it over my head, exposing myself to him.

His eyes grew as hungry as the night before, but I wasn't sure I could do this now. My stomach was nauseous from all the information I'd just found, and my mother sobbing on my bed was playing over and over again in my mind.

He leaned in to kiss me, but I turned my cheek, my arms crossing over my breasts and stomach. His mouth lingered on my cheek. "I'll go cook," he whispered, kissing my cheek softly one more time. "Don't be sad, please."

I didn't answer because there was nothing I could say that wouldn't make him flip his dangerous switch. I stood in the hot water until my fingers were pruned. My mind wouldn't stop reeling, my confidence fading, telling me I wouldn't be able to do this. That I couldn't fake being in love with him, even if doing that meant I could keep a small part of Mitch.

Tears fell when I thought of him, his smile and dimple, those green eyes that penetrated through me, seeing all of my bruises and treating them with a delicateness that no one ever had.

Even though my stomach was growling at me, I didn't want to eat. I didn't want to *feel*. But I had to. I had to pull myself together for Mitch and my family.

Taking a deep breath, I turned off the water and dried off with one of the plush towels Rod left out for me. My instinct was telling me to put something sexy on to continue this game with Rod, but my heart just couldn't do it. I found the drawer with sweats, then blinked for a moment, recalling how his eyes heated when he said he wouldn't allow anyone to see me in one of his T-shirts. I crossed the hall, the light instantly turning on by my motion of entering his closet. Reaching to open a drawer, I rolled my eyes as I noticed it had a thumbprint slot. *Jesus*, he'd thought of everything. Finally, I found an unlocked drawer that held white T-shirts and threw one over my head. It was soft but not as cozy as Mitch's T-shirt. I'd have to pretend I was wearing one of his from now on and not Rod's.

When I walked into the kitchen, Rod was standing at the stove, stirring sauce in a pan. He felt my presence as I sat down at the counter and gave me a wry smile. "Feel better after a shower?"

I nodded, my hands finding my lap. He turned down the stove, then pulled a tray of assorted cheeses and crackers from the fridge and placed them on the counter. "I thought you could use an appetizer."

My shaky hand reached for a cracker, not moving it to my mouth fast enough. The salt tasted amazing, and I reached for another along with a slice of cheese before I finished swallowing the first bite.

Rod smiled as he watched me eat. "I'm making pasta. Do you want a dessert, too?"

I shook my head no, eating another piece of cheese.

After checking the oven once, he grabbed a bottle of wine from the fridge, then pressed his finger to another cupboard, clicking it open so he could grab two wine glasses. My mouth stopped chewing as he filled them with the dark substance.

"I'll just have water."

Rod furrowed his brows as he poured. "Since when do you turn down wine?"

"Since I haven't eaten. I'll get sick."

He stopped pouring, then nodded his head in understanding. "I'm not supposed to drink, but the Doc said one glass every now and then wouldn't do any damage. It'll only make me sleepy."

I blinked at him, now curious what type of medication he was taking. Whatever the prescription was, it wasn't helping how it was supposed to.

He cleared his throat, then dumped both glasses down the drain. "Let's not test those waters tonight." After rinsing the glasses, he dried them and placed them back in the locked cabinet. "I see you wandered to my closet."

I grasped his shirt as I swallowed. "Yes, I wanted something comfortable."

After tossing a mixture of veggies in a pan, he turned to me. "Glad my shirt brings you that."

I grinned. *The stupid fucker.* He actually fell for it. Pretending to be in love with him might be easier to sell than I'd thought.

The crackers and cheese were almost gone by the time he placed a steaming plate of pasta loaded with chicken and veggies stirred with a pesto sauce in front of me. My mouth watered from the smell, and I couldn't wait to eat it.

"Normally we'll eat in the dining room, but you seem cozy here."

I nodded. I doubted I'd ever be cozy in this prison. "I don't remember you cooking," I said after taking my first bite.

He smirked. "Turned into a hobby. I'll cook for you more often this time around. I'll do a lot more for you."

I forced a smile in his direction, but really my smile spurred from memories of Mitch. He was an amazing cook.

"Are you finished? You didn't eat much." Rod frowned.

"Too much cheese and crackers." My stomach was sour now, most likely from fear and guilt.

Rod grabbed my plate and his, proceeding to rummage and clean up the kitchen. I didn't remember him being such a homemaker. He was trying really hard in the most messed up way.

"I'll save some for you to have tomorrow. I'll be gone most of the day." He turned to me with probing eyes. "Can you manage being here without me?"

Keeping a cool expression was difficult. "Why wouldn't I be able to handle myself?"

Rod frowned. "This is a lot to accept so soon."

"Accept? Did I have an option to decline?" The sarcasm was evident in my tone, and Rod's frown deepened. "I think it's obvious you've done everything to keep me inside these walls."

He finished his task, then walked toward me. My body stiffened. Maybe I shouldn't have been snarky with him. He slowly spun my stool so I was facing him, trapping me with is arms on the island counter.

"You *will* stay inside these walls until I know where your heart lies. Freedom will come to you once you make the correct choice."

"How do you know I haven't made that choice already?"

He leaned forward, his breath warm against my cheek. "Because you're as good of a liar as I am, and fucking is easy for you to say yes too." His eyes met mine. "Just because you let me claim you last night doesn't mean you've given me your heart. I've been watching you for years, Jamie. I know when you're speaking from the heart, and when you're playing games."

I swallowed hard, my eyes closing so his blue rays would stop penetrating me. He knew too much about me, almost more than I knew myself. But he never saw me with Mitch behind closed doors, at least not that I could tell. The only cameras were in my room, where Mitch had never been, and the office. I was always a huge bitch to Mitch at work.

My heart beat faster. Why did I treat him so poorly? My ability to have a normal relationship was terrible and Rod knew that. My friendship with Nathan was always true, so Rod had mistaken that for a romantic love. Maybe that's how I'd have to treat Rod? Like he was my friend, not my lover. Because I obviously treated the one I really loved like a piece of shit.

"So I'll be getting an injection in my neck again?" I whispered, leaning into the back of my stool, needing space from Rod.

Rod stood tall, crossing his arms over his chest. "I know you have to trust me, too." He held his hand out for me to take. I eyed it, then reached out, letting him lead me to the couch. A dirty, grimy feeling pricked my entire body when I thought of the moment.

We sat, Rod still holding my hand. "I don't want to drug you."

I didn't want that either. My free hand covered my stomach as I crossed my legs underneath me, trying to find comfort. "I don't know how I could do anything you wouldn't approve of. I mean there are locks everywhere. There's this thing on my leg so you always know where I am. I can't even cook us dinner because all the sharp objects are locked." I let out a slight laugh at his preparation so I wouldn't escape or try to kill him.

He grabbed my chin, forcing me to look at him while his other hand squeezed mine. "It won't always be like this."

We stared at each other for a few moments, trying to read each other's minds. We both were masters of our own games. Maybe this situation was God's punishment for all the bullshit we'd put innocent people who wanted to get close to us through. My shaky hands reached for his cheeks, massaging the stubble that was there. His eyes closed briefly, as though the touch was relaxing for him. I'd have to remember that.

"Not drugging me every day would help with the trust issues."

He nodded without opening his eyes. "I know."

"We have to be friends for anything to work."

His eyelids lifted slowly, wanting to fight the relaxed state he was feeling from my fingers. "I've never had a real friend."

"It's a good thing to have." A lump began to form in my throat. "Becca was my first real friend. But when I think about it, I'm not very good to her." Rod's eyes opened fully, reaching for one of my hands so he could hold it. "I mean, I've always been honest with her, cared about her, but she doesn't know that much about me. No one does."

Except Mitch.

"No one knows me either. You're the only person I've ever talked about my mom too."

I remembered the time at the beach when he talked about her briefly. It was a sore subject, I could tell. She was sick and in a mental hospital. Where her son should be.

"I'm not like her," he whispered as though he could read my thoughts. "She tried to kill me when I was little. It was meant to be a duel suicide." My stomach twisted. "I was seven. She made a cake and dumped her prescription pills in it. I remember them pumping my stomach."

He was so fucked up, and it wasn't totally his fault. "She was sick."

His eyes darted to me. "Would you kill your own son if you had one?"

My arms crossed over my stomach as my scowl deepened, my heart hurting with such a horrible thought.

"I didn't think so." Rod stood, never meeting my eyes. "I have some work to do. You can do what you'd like on the main floor. If you need anything, I'll be in my office."

And he left.

I guess it was safe to say he didn't feel the need to drug me when he was home.

I sat there for a while, dumbfounded. I couldn't let myself feel bad for him, or give him an excuse for kidnapping me and holding me against my will. I needed to find out what meds he was taking. Standing, I moved to the bathroom. Maybe he had his prescriptions in his cabinet. My hand pulled the knob, and of course, it was locked by his handprint. I huffed. It was going to take time to get out of this nightmare.

Searching a few more places was no use. He was good at covering his tracks, and finding a slip up from him so early in the game wasn't going to happen. My curiosity got the better of me, and I roamed the main level of the house on my own. We didn't spend time looking at all of the rooms, and I was surprised to see the fitness room wasn't locked. I could strangle him with a jump rope but, of course, he'd already thought of that. There were no free weights, only cardio equipment.

A workout would do me good since I hadn't moved in a week. My stomach clenched, feeling woozy at the thought of intense movement. I needed to find something to do to take my mind off of this madness, and try to not daydream about Mitch. It hurt my heart too much to think about him and all the love we could have shared.

A tear fell down my cheek as I walked down the hall to a game room. There was a computer, maybe I could get on the internet, email Mitch and tell him where I was? If he'd even want to rescue me after the news reporters made it look like I was involved in trying to kill Nathan.

Nathan. I wanted to know if he was okay. I'd check that out on the computer too. Maybe the news has had more on the story since the last bit I saw the previous night. But, of course, no internet. Only mindless games like Solitaire and Minesweeper.

I flopped down on the couch in front of a flat screen, wrapping myself in the blanket that was draped over the back of the couch. The queasy feeling in my stomach was coming back. I had to pull myself together. Lying and crying on the couch wasn't going to solve anything. And it sure as hell wasn't going to get me out of here.

After wallowing for a while, I went to find Rod in his office. He said to come to him if I needed anything, and besides needing to punch him in the face, I had to make a move to win his game.

Remembering how Rod placed his hand on the screen, I pressed mine against it, surprised that it clicked. Worry washed over me. Maybe he needed his space? He was a ticking time bomb, and me not leaving him be might cause for him to explode. But by how the door opened, I guess he was hoping I'd come visit him. The door was heavy as I pushed it open, and Rod's eyebrows lifted from his computer screen in surprise.

I stood awkwardly in the doorway. "I was going to bring you a drink, but I couldn't get a glass."

Rod rubbed his stubbled jaw. "Yeah, sorry. I'm going to have to figure something out so you can move around the kitchen."

My steps toward him were tentative, but he rolled his chair to face me as I walked around his desk. *What do I do? Sit on his lap?* That's what I would do if it were Mitch.

His hands drummed on the armrests of his chair, waiting for me to speak. My eyes found my hands. *What would a friend say in this situation?* "I was thinking about you after what you said earlier. I wanted to make sure you were okay."

Rod raised a brow. "Of course I'm fine."

"You didn't seem like it."

Rod pinched his brows together in thought, then gave a soft smile. "You're really worried about me?"

"Well, yeah. You seemed upset when you left."

His hand ran through his hair, causing it to stick up slightly. I hated that he looked attractive at this moment, his faded jeans and white shirt reminding me of Mitch.

"I was." He held his hand out for me to take, and I didn't hesitate this time. "I feel better now that you're here." His smile was still in place as he pulled me between his legs.

I timidly rested against his thigh, looking at the computer screen. "What are you working on?"

His hand let go of mine, only to slide across my lower back and to my hip. "Something to make your family feel better. I know it upset you when you saw your mother on the screen."

I'd temporarily forgotten seeing her crying on my bed. My eyes refused to look toward the wall of video surveillance. Rod noticed.

"Your dad came and got her." His hand moved up and down my back. "He said a few things to make her smile."

"He's good at that," I whispered, running my fingers under my eyes to stop a tear from falling.

We were quiet for a moment, the stillness bringing visions of my parents happily in love. They were always so affectionate toward each other.

"There's something that I've kept from you for too long," Rod murmured, both his hands wrapped around my waist now.

"Only one thing?" He scowled at my sarcasm. "Sorry."

He shook his head and smiled. "I know, I know. You've got a bit more fire than you used to. I like it."

I rolled my eyes, causing him to chuckle.

He became serious again. "I know you think it was my fault your dad lost his job with the police department." My back stiffened, causing his hand to still. His jaw ticked once he realized he had my full attention. "It wasn't totally my fault."

I scowled at him.

Letting out a deep sigh, he continued. "When I first started, I came to your father's office early and unexpectedly to get some paperwork signed. His secretary wasn't at her desk, but I didn't think anything of it."

My stomach sank. Where was he going with this?

"His secretary was with him in his office."

"So...?"

Rod frowned, his eyes squinting uncomfortably. "They weren't working, Jamie."

My jaw dropped. "Are you saying my father and the secretary had a thing?"

Rod cocked his head, his frown deepening.

I wanted to smack him, tell him to fuck off for making up stupid shit. But I didn't, I stayed there, his arms wrapped around my waist protectively.

"I knew it'd crush you, and probably crush your view on love. I didn't want to hurt you with that kind of information. But when you left me that night, I was so angry. I set up a video camera in his office. I was going to show you the video because I was so mad, but I did something worse."

My voice was barely a whisper. "You showed your grandfather."

He hung his head in shame. "He said your dad needed to resign or it'd hit the news."

That's what our "little secret" was going to be. My dad thought I knew about his affair with his secretary, and didn't want me to tell my mother. Both hands rubbed my eyes, not wanting to believe any of this, but it made sense. There were signs. My parents' marriage struggled for a while after Rod and my affair, and all that time I thought it was because of me. That I'd ruined my dad's career by screwing around with a man who was older than me. But it was because of my father's selfish decisions.

"I always blamed myself," I whispered. "Why would he do that to my mom?"

Rod squeezed me tighter, pulling me so I was sitting in his lap. I was shell shocked as he kissed my temple and cheeks affectionately. "I don't know, baby. I'm so sorry I told on him. I know that only pushed you away from me more."

"He must have told her. They weren't on good terms for a while. I always thought they fought over my careless decisions. It got worse when Landon died. I guess I just assumed..." I was stuttering, my words not making any sense. I wanted Mitch. He'd understand. His father was a sleazeball and screwed his mom over dozens of times. Knowing that part of his father tugged at me even more.

"No, your dad isn't like that. Both of them would never blame their problems on you or Landon." Rod's hand ran through my hair as I stared blankly at the surveillance screens. I didn't like how Landon's name sounded coming from his lips. I turned my head from his touch, needing distance, but knowing I couldn't completely push him away. "Landon was never supposed to die," he confessed after I flinched away from him. "That night's still a blur. I only wanted you to talk to me." His hand pressed firmer on my back, his other arm staying snug around my waist. "No one was supposed to get hurt."

"But they did. You might not have meant to kill Landon, but what about his best friend?"

"Kevin killed himself. He was driving the car, not me."

I shook my head, knowing Rod believed his own lies. Kevin had severe head trauma and was found in the driver's seat of the car. I knew Rod had beat him, then used his body as a dummy for the car crash. His grandfather knew too, but because of his position in the police department, Rod got away with murder, *again*.

Both of Rod's arms pulled me to his chest, his nose nuzzling my arm. Did he need affection for this? All of this was his fault. Even if my father really had an affair with his secretary, I was willing to blame it on Rod. He'd ruined my life. Why not blame all of my problems on him?

I let out a huge breath of air, the guilt and grief of my brother intermingling with the guilt I felt for Nathan in the hospital, and the shame of sleeping with the monster because I thought I had to. Because sleeping with Rod meant I'd be on his side, that he'd be satisfied with keeping me, and not hurting the people I loved.

If giving up my freedom was the cost to keep my loved ones safe, then being bound and shackled to my deepest and darkest nightmare the rest of life would be well worth the torture.

I never wanted to cry in front of Rod, show him my weaknesses, but if he wanted to think he was manipulating me, maybe my tears were the ticket to his satisfaction. "I miss him so much," I sniffed, my salty tears yearning for more than just my brother, but for Mitch.

"Baby," he sighed as my body relaxed into his. "Losing your brother must have been such a terrible experience."

My arms wrapped around his neck as his mouth gave gentle kisses to my forehead and cheeks. My body began to tremble. I wanted Mitch to hold me so badly.

"It was awful. I watched him die in my lap. I tried so hard to get out."

"I should have come to you, I should have pulled you out," he admitted, his hand running up and down my shuddering body. "I've only ever wanted to make my mistakes right with you. I'll do everything in my power to keep you safe, to turn your tears of sadness into joy. To make you forget every horrible memory I've put you through."

His breath was warm on my neck, and I scrunched my shoulders, shying away. I didn't want him to touch me there, it was too painful. He wasn't allowed to mend that wound he dug so deep inside of me. Dry lips hesitated, then a heavy breath released from his mouth.

"I love you so much, Jamie."

He bravely pressed his mouth behind my ear, firmer than the sweet kisses on my cheeks and forehead. I closed my eyes to the touch, pleading for my brain to picture Mitch's firm lips healing me, his bulky arms surrounding me, that the shallow breaths from Rod were the air from Mitch.

Rod thought he'd won me over and manipulated me again. I wouldn't share with him how his words were like venom. How I'd imagined another man's hand and lips were in place of his. He was bringing me comfort now, and I was going to let him think he relaxed me, made me feel safe when I was really more scared than I'd ever been.

Rod's mouth continued to press along my jaw, his hands creeping under my shirt. "No other woman could satisfy my thirst for you, you know that right?" he whispered, his lips catching the corner of my mouth. I looked into his lust-filled eyes. "I'd never betray you like that. I'll never betray you ever again."

I let him kiss me, my heart shattering as I betrayed the one I loved.

CHAPTER SEVENTEEN

Mitch

"I don't believe it."

Hendry sighed at my stubbornness.

"That's not her."

"Her parents sure think it is."

I huffed as I sat down in the chair across from Hendry, rubbing both my eyes with my palms. The enlarged, blurry photo stills from a surveillance camera he placed in front of me just couldn't be Jamie.

"The camera footage I searched all have stills of her car at this port. I'm sorry, Mitch, but there comes a time when—"

"When what?" I snapped. "This is horse shit. Someone is framing her. That's not Jamie!"

The woman was dressed in the same clothing as the woman in the video surveillance Hendry found from a shop outside of Plaza Towers the day Nathan was attacked and Jamie went missing.

"Look. I can't touch someone once they cross the border. We'll keep a close eye on this location, but I think it's safe to say Jamie is fleeing the crime scene."

"Jamie wouldn't try to kill my brother!" This was maddening. I couldn't take it. No one seemed to be on my side. And those letters from the crazy stalker weren't being taken seriously enough.

"Do you know where the ship was going?" I sighed. "I'll go look for her myself."

Hendry shook his head. "I tried to get the records from the shipyard on possible destinations, but it seems his book-keeping is behind. That ship could have gone to multiple places that day. I think searching islands would be a waste of your time."

"Searching for Jamie would never be a waste of time."

Hendry was getting frustrated. "I know you don't want to think the worst of your girlfriend, but you need to let it go."

"I can't *let it go*. And I don't think your supervisor would approve you letting this case go either," I challenged, my anger evident.

His eyes narrowed as he met my glare. "I'm not letting it go, but YOU need to. This will destroy you if you stay hung up on this woman. You obviously didn't know her very well at all."

I ground my teeth, then left his office. Fuck him. I was going to see Ryan and find out what he really thought of this information. Surely he'd know his daughter well enough to realize that blurry image wasn't her. Even if the hair color and body type were similar.

I jumped in my truck and slammed the door, firing up the engine. It had been a week since Hendry spoke publicly about Nathan's attacker and Jamie's disappearance. Unfortunately, the media was on Hendry's side. They thought she'd tried to kill him.

They were fucking morons.

"Can you meet me?" I asked Ryan when he picked up his phone. It was nearing seven at night, and I was already turning on the highway to get to Point Canal where Jamie's parents lived. I knew it killed them to be so far away, but they had a family to raise.

Ryan sighed. "Take it Hendry showed you the new photos from the port."

"It's not her." Ryan was silent. "I'm heading there now." I hung up before he could respond. Her family didn't need to be doubting her now, too.

"Hey, Mitch," Leslie greeted as I walked up the steps to their house. I embraced her with a hug that she so obviously needed.

"I'll heat up some leftovers for you," she said with kindness, although sadness filled her eyes. "How's Nathan?"

"Still no change. My mom's been by his side twenty-four-seven."

"I'm sorry to hear he hasn't gotten better."

"Mitch!" Jamie's twin brothers greeted, running to me and nearly tackling me in the process. "Did you come to play games with us again? I want a rematch in Madden!" Collin said, or at least I thought it was Collin and not Jacob. I still couldn't tell the two of them apart.

"I'm not sure if you'll have time for a game," Leslie said, shooing the boys away from me. "It's almost time for bed."

"Mom," they groaned simultaneously.

She waved them in the direction of the bathroom. "Go, shower, brush your teeth, get your jammies on, and then we'll see."

They hurried along, shoving each other to get there first.

"Sorry, I didn't think about interrupting their routine when I decided to drive down here."

She shook her head. "Never be sorry for coming to visit us."

Riley, Jamie's sister, emerged from the kitchen. She looked upset and I assumed they'd been keeping her in the loop about Jamie to a point. She offered me a slight smile, then walked down the hall.

"Forgive her, she's been watching the news too much. I think schools been hard for her lately because of all this."

My shoulders tensed. I'm sure kids made the connection between Jamie on the news and Riley. I bet they all believed the reporters. Poor girl. I was tempted to go to school and show all those little punks a thing or two about gossip.

"Trevor's been holed up in his room since it all happened," Leslie choked. "The twins don't know what's going on. We try to keep them away from the news, but the older ones know how to search the internet."

"Leslie, don't believe them. You know your daughter would never hurt anyone," I pleaded. She offered me a grateful smile as she removed plastic wrap from a plate and popped it into a microwave.

"Mitch, you really didn't have to come all the way here," Ryan said as he walked into the small kitchen. He looked just as beat up as Leslie did.

"I wanted to give you this." I pulled out an envelope from my back pocket and handed it to Ryan. "I found it in Jamie's room."

Ryan glanced at me skeptically, then thumbed through the envelope, finding a stack of twenties. "You didn't have to do this, Mitch."

"I didn't do anything. I just found it and figured Jamie wanted you to have it. What is it, anyway?" I lied. I put the money inside and tried to write Mom and Dad in Jamie's handwriting on the front.

"Jamie always writes checks," he sighed, tossing the envelope on the counter, then grabbed two beers from the fridge and handed one to me. "You don't have to take care of us."

I took the beer, feeling awkward. "I know, but it was important to Jamie."

Ryan smiled, nodding his head toward the porch for me to join him. "I'll bring your food outside when it's done," Leslie said, pushing me to go with Ryan.

"You've got a keeper there." I grinned at Ryan. He smirked back as we took a seat on the porch furniture. "That I do. I've fought hard to keep her, that's for sure."

"You've obviously done something right." I sighed, feeling like I'd failed Jamie. I knew she wasn't the type of girl who would heat up leftovers for me, but she was the one I wanted to keep in my life.

"Stop beating yourself up over this," Ryan scolded, patting my knee. "Jamie is a free bird, like me. It's not easy to tame her. Lord knows she doesn't let anyone in... She also gets that from me."

"I used to be like that," I said quietly, sipping my beer. "Until I met her." I felt so raw, so cut open. Jamie was my one and only saving grace. I knew she cared about me, and I knew she was in trouble. "We have to find her. Something deep inside of me is telling me she didn't run, that she's being forced to stay away from us."

Ryan offered me a sympathetic smile. "I feel that same way, but those photos..." Ryan gulped. "They sure look like her." The tone in his voice proved he felt the same way as

Leslie. He closed his eyes briefly. "Jamie normally needs time to figure things out. She'll come back around if she left on purpose, but I think you're right. I can't help but feel she's close by. I don't think she's being hurt, at least not yet. Whoever wrote those letters you found cares deeply for her, and I've been pressing my memory, trying to remember if there were any signs of crazy guys chasing her behind my back while she was growing up."

"Can you think of any?" I asked with hope. "The name Rod really doesn't ring a bell?"

Frustrated, he shook his head. "No, I've run that name through my head a million times since seeing those letters. Jamie took her brother to prom, so I'm thinking it'd have to have been someone in college who she kept from us. Unless it was someone she's never met, but from what some of those letters said, it sure seems like they'd been together in the past. I'm so mad at myself for not being more observant. You'd think I'd have kept a closer eye on my daughter."

"This isn't your fault, either," I reassured him.

Leslie brought the plate of food out to me with a smile. I could tell she didn't want to talk about this mess.

"I'm debating going to the islands."

Ryan frowned. "Don't do that. Like I said, I feel like she's somewhere close. We just need to keep our eyes open. Besides, if Jamie's on an island, it means she needs to be alone, and that we should leave her."

I chugged the rest of my beer, frustrated with Ryan's thoughts. I understood what he was saying, but I wasn't willing to wait.

CHAPTER EIGHTEEN

Jamie

Heaving into the toilet was my new wake-up routine. It was nearing a month being locked in this mansion. Rod would come and go, along with the foreign workers. They never met my eyes, only did their tasks of cleaning and cooking. I still wasn't allowed to access anything. I was surprised Rod gave me a toothbrush. *Maybe I could shove it so far in his ear that it would scratch his brains and knock some sense into him.*

Rod was in a fantasy world, worshiping my every move. He'd be any woman's dream. Except I knew the real him, and it was scratching at the surface. I knew he was on the verge of switching, turning into the dark demon that wanted to control my purpose in life. Thankfully, he'd stopped drugging me.

I knew I wouldn't be able to hide my secret from him forever. My body would begin changing, and by how Rod's hands roamed, he'd notice right away.

I hated sleeping with him. I hated kissing him like I wanted him. When my body would tremble, it was because I'd pictured Mitch, his hands and warmth moving inside of me, not Rod's. The guilt was overwhelming now. I could imagine Mitch was the one making me feel good a million times in my head, but when I opened my eyes, it was always Rod, staring at me with lust, kissing me like he needed me to breath. My soul was stolen, and the only thing keeping me from crawling into a deep, dark hole was the smallest part of Mitch growing inside of me.

Thanksgiving was gut wrenching. Rod tried to make it pleasant, cooking a big dinner, setting the table, trying to make the holiday warm as though we were our own family. I put on a face for him, letting him know I was grateful for his holiday cheer, but I was dying inside.

It was Christmas Eve now, and I craved being with my family. All of us together on Christmas constantly reminded me how important family was. We'd play games and sing, love surrounding us, and I wasn't there. Instead, I sat in the monster's living room on the couch, dressed in a black cocktail dress with my hair curled and makeup covering the dark rims under my eyes. I wanted to kick off my heels, but Rod wanted me to wear them. He probably had some creepy fantasy that involved me wearing shoes. I shuddered at the thought.

"I made my grandfather's famous eggnog," Rod said with a smile as he came to sit next me on the white couch. One of his housekeepers was nice enough to set up Christmas decorations, including a giant tree with garland and bulbs. It was the most beautiful thing I'd seen since being in this hell hole.

Rod handed me a glass, then sat down, putting his arm behind the back of the couch where I was sitting, his thigh touching my knee. "Cheers."

We clinked glasses and sipped. The moment my glass left my lips, his face moved forward, his mouth pressing against mine smoothly. He wanted more from the kiss, but I just couldn't do it tonight. I couldn't fake being happy on Christmas Eve when I was being kept from the ones I loved.

Rod sighed as he pulled back, his blond locks swept past his forehead as he studied me. "Come on, let's dance."

I set my eggnog on the coffee table, smoothing my tight cocktail dress down my hips. Rod watched my every move, his eyes growing hungrier when they reached my black heels.

"You've always had the best legs," his husky voice said as one hand snaked around my waist, pulling me to his chest. My hands found his arms, my eyes not meeting his. The sadness was woeful, sucking up every part of me. I didn't want to feel so miserable, but not knowing what my loved ones were doing was torture.

Rod's hands found my cheeks, tilting my head toward his. My eyelids stayed half-closed, not wanting to make a connection with him. "Who are you thinking about?"

I bit the insides of my cheeks and moved my hands so they were behind his neck. Couldn't we just be silent? Couldn't he just dance with me, fuck me, and fall asleep? I wanted a night off as an actress.

"Come on, baby, it's Christmas Eve. I want our first *real* Christmas together to be memorable."

"It will be," I choked. *No*. I couldn't lose myself in front of him.

Rod's hands left my cheeks and moved to my waist, gently guiding me to move in a rhythm with him to the soft Christmas music playing from the stereo. "It'd help if you'd smile," he coaxed in my ear. "I love getting a genuine grin from those delectable lips."

I gulped, my lips quivering as I tried my hardest to raise them, but instead a tear rolled down my cheek.

"Tell me what's on your mind." I stayed silent. "I won't get upset." My head only moved slightly to the side.

Rod sighed in frustration and stopped swaying. His hands moved back to my cheeks, his grasp firmer this time, causing my eyes to flicker open wide. The blue of his eyes was icy, becoming angrier with each passing moment. This was it. He was about to flip. I'd been lucky it took him this long to turn into a monster.

"Why are you thinking about him?" he asked through clenched teeth. "Why won't you forget about him?"

My eyes closed painfully. I could never forget about Mitch. But he was talking about Nathan, and I hadn't forgotten about him either. The fear of him not waking was always on my mind.

"I'm not." I lied.

"You must forget about him," he demanded.

"He was my friend," I said softly. "I only want to know if he's okay."

Rod moved us, his thumbs rubbing roughly along my cheeks as he backed me into the wall. His hips were pressed against mine now. I could feel his tension and anger.

"You need to forget about him."

Tears pressed against my eyes as anger burned inside of me. "I'll never forget about him."

Rod cocked his head, his hands moving to the base of my neck as his lip curled. "You really should."

"Why? Because you don't want me to constantly compare him to you?" His eyes widened in shock at my words. "You don't want me to think about him while you're taking off my clothes, pretending your hands are his?"

Rod's thumbs began to press into my neck, and I almost wanted him to strangle me. I was nearing the point where suffocating would be better than never living my own life outside of Rod's world.

"Is that what you do? You think of his cock inside of you? His mouth never worshiped you like mine. He never sated you the way I do. He doesn't know how to make you feel like you're on fire." Rod's harsh whisper increased to yelling as his hands pressed further, jamming into my airway.

My voice was raspy as I began to shake. "Rod... I can't... breathe..."

His eyes were wild as my mouth gaped open in search for air. Then I saw it, the same excitement in his eyes as when he'd choked me so many nights before. The way his pupils dilated and his breathing sped faster with each gasp for air I took. His hands finally released my throat, one clutching my jaw while the other pulled the hair from my nape. "You're *mine*. Do you understand? Stop fucking thinking about him. You only think about me now."

Falling to my knees, tears sprung from my eyes as my chest expanded from inhaling big drags of oxygen. He knelt down with me, never letting go of my face or hair. I fucking hated Rod. "I'll never stop thinking about him!"

"Well, he's dead, sweetheart."

My eyes shot up to his. "What?"

His words were like venom as he hissed his breath across my cheek. "He didn't wake up. He died from cardiac arrest. I didn't want to tell you, but if that's the only way you'll fucking forget about him, then so be it."

A loud, uncontrollable sob escaped me as my fist flew to Rod's chest. "You killed my best friend!"

"No, you did," he snarled, grabbing my hands and pinning me to the floor so I was underneath him.

I squirmed against his strong frame, still fighting him. He needed to get the hell away from me. "You kill everyone I love!"

"He was in the way. He wasn't any good for you. I couldn't let you be with that cocky leech of a business man."

"You moron!" I shouted. "I didn't love him like that."

Rod held my wrists on either side of my head, slightly sitting up and straddling me. I had his full attention now as he scowled down at me.

"He was my best friend. Not my lover," my voice quivered in pain, "We were never intimate. He didn't desire me that way. He didn't even like women. He was gay." The reality that he was dead hit me like a train. My angry outburst turned into wretched tears. I stopped thrashing, only crying more.

I'd killed Mitch's brother.

Now he'd never forgive me.

FOLLOW BROOKE PAGE:

FACEBOOK

TWITTER

INSTAGRAM

THE CONCLUSION OF

THE OBSESSION SERIES

ACKNOWLEDGEMENTS

Now this is always the hard part, because I never know where to start, and well, I tend to ramble.

First, I need to thank my loving husband. All those nights when you were okay with letting me escape to the coffee shop to finish this book will never be forgotten. I love you more and more every day, and am grateful for your constant support and faith in me. You make my dreams become a reality everyday.

My family, who have been supportive from day one. You cheer me on, talk about me to your friends, and only wish for me to succeed. I love you all dearly.

My darling Tonya. I don't know what I'd do without you. You keep me on my game and are always throwing me in the right direction. We've become an awesome team, and best friends. Why must you live so far away? I look forward to our phone calls and count down the days until we will see each other again.

Jen- Thank God I found you! You've helped polish my writing, and I'm flabbergasted by your talent. Not only are you extremely talented at what you do, you're an amazing friend as well. I love that I can message you about so much more than just my books.

Brooke's Babes, thank you for your constant support. I love every single one of you and your everlasting faith in my as a writer. Whenever I feel like quitting, you ladies lift me up, and I can't express how much that means to me. Babes for life!

My lovely beta readers: Sara, Amanda, Angela, Ashley, Amber, Tenise- your feedback was beyond helpful and I am so appreciative that you all took your time out to give me your thoughts on how to make HIDE as good as it can be!

Amanda Maxlyn, my author bestie. Our phone calls could be never ending, and I'm always smiling whenever I receive a message from you (all forms, snapchats, messenger, texts, even voicemails.) You're an outstanding author and I'm thankful we can bounce ideas and have a trusting relationship with our writing. I know I can tell you anything and everything, and you'll only judge me a little, lol!

Dana Leah, you've blown me away with your design talent. The cover and teasers for Hide are breath taking. Thank you for helping to paint a picture for Hide, and for many more works to come!

Jen Wildner, I wanted to put a derogatory term here, but some might not get our humor. Thanks for being so amazing and helping spread the word about HIDE. You are truly selfless and have the kindest heart. Just One More Page is by far the

BEST blog out there because an amazing woman is behind it! Love you boo!

Kellie and the Eye Candy Book Store team- Every time I open my Twitter feed I'm astounded by your support! Not only there, but everywhere else Eye Candy! Your promotion is spectacular and I'm proud to call myself an Eye Candy Author!

Emmy Hamilton, my Canadian lover and amazing proof reader! Our convos are close to my heart, and I only wish we could talk on the phone more! (Dang long distance phone calls!) Your confidence inspires me, and I hope to be that way one day!

Stacy Leier- Heeeeeeey....My last minute lifesaver! Not many people will drop what they're doing to give a book a final look! Thank you so much chica!

A huge shout out to all of the blogs we have participated in my tour! Authors would be nothing without bloggers!

Last but not least, my Beachbody coach, Casey. You may not be in the writing world, but you're helping me to find myself. Your inspiration and faith in me has contributed to my writing in such a wonderful way. I'm so proud to have you as my coach on this life journey of mine.

ABOUT THE AUTHOR

Brooke Page is an independent author focusing on contemporary and suspenseful romance. She and her husband live with their two children in the suburbs of Grand Rapids, Michigan. When she's not writing about steamy alpha males, she enjoys all types of art, including painting, drawing, and pottery. She also loves a good book, and can be found reading on her phone at any spare minute.